FEAR STREET
R·L·STINE

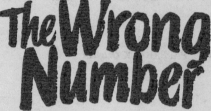

The Wrong Number

AN ARCHWAY PAPERBACK
Published by POCKET BOOKS
New York   London   Toronto   Sydney   Tokyo   Singapore

This book is a work of fiction. Names, characters, places and incidents are either the product of the author's imagination or are used fictitiously. Any resemblance to actual events or locales or persons, living or dead, is entirely coincidental.

AN ARCHWAY PAPERBACK *Original*

An Archway Paperback published by
POCKET BOOKS, a division of Simon & Schuster Inc.
1230 Avenue of the Americas, New York, NY 10020

ISBN: 0-671-69411-1

First Archway Paperback printing March 1990

15   14   13   12

IL 6+

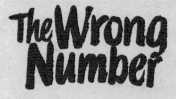

prologue

S cheming. It was the thing he'd been best at in his life. Seeing something he wanted, and figuring out how to go after it, step by step.

Sure, he messed up a lot. He'd had some bad luck. Sometimes people got in his way. Ruined his perfect plans.

That wouldn't happen this time.

This plan was his best. No way it could fail. No way he'd let anyone mess up this one.

As he sat in the dark, rolling it over and over in his mind, a sneer formed on his face. It was too bad what he had to do. He didn't really want to hurt anyone.

But what choice did he have? He had to take care of himself. No one else was going to take care of him. He'd learned that early, beginning with his parents.

Now he knew it was time to act, and not think about what had happened to him in the past.

After all, it wasn't his fault that he was always getting in trouble.

That was going to change. From now on things would go exactly the way he wanted them to.

He'd made the perfect plan. On the surface, everything seemed normal.

But someone was due for a big surprise.

A deadly surprise.

All he had to do was be patient. Be patient and wait until it was time to act . . .

chapter

1

The First Week in September

*T*he blob of green gel oozed like something from the bottom of a decaying swamp. It spread and settled in its container, quivering, as if searching for a way to escape or a way to take over.

Deena Martinson plunged her hand into the porcelain sink and slowly squeezed in the gelatinous mass.

"Yuck!" she said. "Are you sure you want to put this on your hair?"

"Go ahead," said her friend Jade Smith. Jade was sitting on a wooden stool in front of the bathroom mirror, a towel covering her shoulders, her freshly washed auburn hair hanging in damp coils down her back.

"I know your mom's a professional hairdresser," said Deena, "but this stuff looks like the thing that ate Cincinnati. And I won't even tell you what it feels like."

"Go on," Jade insisted. "My mom uses it on her hair all the time, and it looks great. All shiny and full of body."

"Are you sure you don't mean *dead* bodies?" cracked Deena. She began applying the gel to her friend's hair. Soon the long tresses were covered with slime and gave off a faintly Jell-O-y scent.

"Now what?" she asked when she had finished.

"Now we wait for it to dry," said Jade. "At which point I'll be ravishing. Sure you don't want to try it? We could do your hair in spikes."

Deena fingered her own baby-fine hair. It was short-ish, and blondish, and straightish. All she could do was wear it layered and hope for the best. Her mother said her hairdo made her look like an angel. She wasn't sure she liked that idea, but spikes didn't sound any better. "No, thanks," she said. "I have enough problems without trying secret formula x-oh-nine or whatever it is."

"It could be your big chance," said Jade, but she didn't push, she didn't seem to care much. In fact, she sounded a little bored—as bored as Deena felt.

"What a way to spend Saturday night," said Deena with a sigh.

"Yeah, I hate to admit it," said Jade, "but I'll actually be glad when school starts Monday. It'll be great to see all the kids, start going to dances and games."

"Yeah, I guess," said Deena.

"Hey, Miss Enthusiasm."

"It's just I don't know what to expect," Deena said. "Things are going to be different."

"What do you mean?"

"I just found out that my brother Chuck is going to be living here."

"Your brother? You don't have a brother," said Jade.

"My half-brother, actually. He's my dad's son from his first marriage. I've only met him a few times. He's coming to Shadyside for his senior year."

"Really?" Jade was all ears now, but then she usually was where boys were concerned.

"Down, girl," said Deena. "Chuck is nothing but trouble. In fact, that's why he's coming here. He was supposed to graduate from Central City last year, but he got expelled. His mom and my dad decided he'd do better in a small town like Shadyside."

"Expelled?" said Jade. "What for?"

"I'm not sure," said Deena. "It had something to do with some kids he hung out with. He actually got arrested one time. He's been getting in trouble ever since he was little."

"He sounds interesting," said Jade with a mischievous smile.

"To you, Freddy Krueger would sound interesting," cracked Deena, wandering into her bedroom.

"It's just that the regular boys at Shadyside are so predictable," said Jade, following her. "That's 'predictable,' spelled *B-O-R-I-N-G*." She pulled the towel off her shoulders, then shook her damp hair out and pirouetted in front of the full-length mirror on Deena's closet door, admiring her figure. She was wearing a pink- and white-checked jumpsuit with short sleeves. Deena had heard that redheads weren't supposed to wear pink, but Jade looked good in every color of the rainbow—and she knew it. In fact, she was very vain.

But, Deena had to admit, Jade had a lot to be vain about.

"How's your hair doing?" Deena asked to change the subject.

"Still cooking," said Jade. She suppressed a yawn, then sat on Deena's bed and began using an emery board on her already perfect nails. She looked around the room, her eyes stopping on a bright blue plastic object on the bedside table.

"What's this?" she said.

"My new phone," said Deena. "When my dad got promoted to vice-president of the phone company they gave us the latest instruments."

"It's pretty rad," said Jade, picking it up. "It looks like the control panel for a jet plane or something. What are all these buttons for?"

"They're for programming in phone numbers," said Deena. "You push one button and the phone automatically dials a number. That button's for putting the caller on hold. And this switch"—she pointed to a switch on the handset—"turns it into a speaker phone, so everyone in the room can hear the conversation."

"Yeah?" said Jade. "That sounds like it has possibilities. In fact, it gives me an idea. Whose numbers are in it?"

"I haven't programmed in too many yet," said Deena. "Just my grandmother, Mrs. Weller next door, and you, of course."

"Me? Really? How do I dial it?"

"Just punch number three."

"Watch this. My little sister Cathy's baby-sitting the kids tonight." She punched number three, then flipped the switch for the speaker, a strange smile on her face.

"Hello," she said, holding her nose so she sounded as if she had a cold. "Miss Cathy Smith, please."

"This is Cathy Smith," said the voice on the other end. Through the speaker her voice sounded hollow and far away, as if it were coming from the bottom of a well.

"I'm calling from the Division Street Mall Association," said Jade, still holding her nose. "Miss Smith, I regret to inform you that you have been selected worst-dressed shopper of the month."

"What?" shrieked Cathy at the other end. "I didn't even go to the mall today!"

"You were positively identified by over a dozen shoppers," said Jade. "You have exactly one hour to pick up your prize, a dozen wilted daisies."

"A dozen what?" wailed Cathy. Then her voice turned suspicious. "Wait a minute. I know who this is. It's not the mall. Jade, I know you—"

"I don't know what you're talking about," said Jade, pinching her nose even tighter. "This is the—"

"You can't fool me," Cathy went on. "Next time pick on someone as stupid as you are!" The sound of the click as she hung up filled the room.

"Rats!" said Jade. "I should try it with someone who doesn't know my voice so well. Someone who would never expect—I've got it! Deena, look up Henry Raven's phone number."

"Henry Raven?" said Deena. "He's such a nerd! All he cares about is his computer. Why do you want to talk to him?"

"Just watch," said Jade. "Or rather, listen—to this!" She took the phone book from Deena and punched in seven digits. The sound of a ringing phone filled the room, then a click, and then the unmistakable voice of Henry Raven.

"Hello?"

"Hello, is this Henry?" Jade was talking so low she was almost whispering, and Deena thought her voice sounded mysterious and sexy.

"This is Henry," said Henry. "Who is this?"

"You don't know me, Henry," whispered Jade, "but I've had my eye on you for a long time." She whispered *long* so it sounded like "lo-o-o-ng," her voice breathy and seductive.

"Who *is* this?"

"Someone . . . who'd like to be a good friend. I like your style, Henry—"

"Is this some kind of a joke?"

"It's no joke," said Jade. "I've never been more serious. You're just the kind of guy a girl like me yearns for. . . ."

There was a long silence at the other end. Then suddenly Henry sputtered, "Find another guy! I don't have time for this!" and he hung up the phone with a bang.

Both girls fell on the bed, laughing hysterically.

"Did you hear that? He doesn't have *time!*" Deena couldn't stop giggling.

"That was even better than I expected," said Jade when she stopped laughing. "Now it's your turn."

"My turn?" said Deena.

"Sure. You heard me. We'll just pick—"

"Jade, no!" said Deena. "I can't even talk to people in person!"

"That's the whole point," said Jade. "It's much easier when you're anonymous. Now, let's see," she went on, flipping through Deena's phone book. "How about Rob Morell?"

"Rob Morell?" shrieked Deena. "He's one of the most popular boys in the whole school!"

"So what?" said Jade. "You like him, don't you?"

"Sure," said Deena, "but when he was in my geometry class last year I could never think of anything to say to him."

"Well, now's your chance," Jade said.

"But what if he finds out it's me?"

"Just whisper, like I did, and he won't have a clue," said Jade. Ignoring Deena's continuing protests, she punched in the number and thrust the phone at her friend.

"But what'll I *say?*" cried Deena, looking horrified.

"Whatever comes to your mind," said Jade. "Just be sexy."

"Hello?" squeaked Deena. Then she took a deep breath and dropped her voice. "May I speak to Rob Morell, please?"

Great! Jade mouthed the word. After a moment a sleepy-sounding boy's voice came over the speaker: "Hello?"

"Hello, Rob?" whispered Deena, making her voice as seductive as possible. "What's a good-looking guy like you doing home on a Saturday night?"

"I rented some movies," Rob said. "Who is this?"

"This is your secret admirer," said Deena. The words just came to her.

"My what? What's your name?"

"I can't tell you my name, because then it wouldn't be secret anymore." Deena was amazed at herself. So far the words came easily, as if she were reading them from a script.

"Well, if you can't tell me your name, tell me what you look like," said Rob. He no longer sounded sleepy. In fact, he was sounding interested!

Deena shut her eyes and leaned back on the bed. "What do I look like?" she repeated. "Well, I'm about five four, one hundred and five pounds, with blond hair to my waist. My eyes are green, and I have full lips. People tell me I look like Kim Basinger."

"Say, maybe we could get together sometime," said Rob.

"I'd like that," said Deena. "You're such a good-looking guy. I'll call you again one night real soon."

"How about tonight?" said Rob. "Or tomorrow? Can I have your number?"

"I've got to go now," said Deena. "Remember, I'll call again."

She leaned forward to hang up the phone and looked at Jade a moment. They collapsed back on the bed, shrieking with laughter. "He bought it!" cried Deena. "I can't believe it! He was practically drooling!"

"You were great!" said Jade. "You're a natural. He'll probably stay home waiting by the phone for the next month!"

"You were right," said Deena. "It was easy. Much easier than talking to someone in person."

"I told you so," said Jade. "So who should we call next? How about—"

"Not tonight," said Deena, looking at her watch. "It's getting late, and my folks will be home any minute."

"What about tomorrow?" said Jade.

Deena shook her head. "Tomorrow night my dad and I are driving to the airport to pick up my brother Chuck."

"Be sure to tell him hello for me," said Jade.

"He doesn't even know you."

Jade turned her full smile on. "Not now he doesn't," she said. "But I have a feeling . . . he will soon."

chapter

2

*O*n the way to the airport Deena felt both excited and nervous. She was beginning to like the idea of having a long-lost brother in the house. In fact, she realized, there could be certain important advantages—such as he could introduce her to his friends. Then she'd remember everything she'd heard about the trouble Chuck had been in. She got a funny feeling in the pit of her stomach that maybe things weren't going to work out so well.

Also, her father seemed really nervous, even more nervous than she was.

"Be friendly to him, Deena," her dad said. "But try to give him space. Remember, he grew up in a big city and isn't used to small-town friendliness."

"Right," said Deena. He'll probably think we're all a bunch of hicks, she thought.

Her first glimpse of Chuck was promising. She

hadn't seen him since he was about ten, and he'd grown up since then. He was tall now, and his T-shirt and tight jeans showed off the taut muscles of an athlete. His hair was thick and sandy above startlingly blue eyes. Jade, Deena knew, would call Chuck a hunk. But when she got closer she saw that something was wrong with the picture of the all-American good-looking guy.

For one thing, there was the expression on his face.

Deena wasn't sure what it was. It seemed to be somewhere between a scowl and a sneer. A snowl? she wondered.

When Deena's father put out his hand for a hand-shake, Chuck pretended he didn't see it. Mr. Martin-son looked a little flustered and smiled uncertainly. "Chuck, you remember your sister Deena."

Chuck looked at her as if she were a toad or some other low form of life. "Hello, kid," he said.

Kid? This year was going to be awful, Deena knew. But in the next instant Chuck smiled at her, a goofy, lopsided smile that made him look like a completely different person. She smiled back nervously, wonder-ing what to expect next.

On the way home it was even more confusing. Deena sat in the backseat and listened while her father and Chuck talked.

Except it was mostly her father talking. Chuck just grunted. Once he said, "This is such a drag, man. I don't see why I can't go back to Central City High."

"Because they won't let you back in," said Mr. Martinson. "Your mother and I have repeatedly talked to them, as you well know." For the first time Deena's father sounded a little exasperated, maybe even angry.

Deena hoped to hear more about why Chuck had been expelled. "I want to make clear to you—" her father started.

But the sound of squealing brakes and screeching tires interrupted him.

Deena screamed at the sound of the crash.

She heard glass shattering. Then another crash.

A horn started honking, then another. Someone cried out.

More tires squealed. Deena held her hands over her ears.

Mr. Martinson, a look of horror on his face, his mouth wide open, stomped on the brakes. His tan BMW skidded toward a jumble of other cars and came to a stop just inches from the car in front of it. Behind them Deena could hear more cars sliding and skidding. "Get out!" Mr. Martinson ordered. "It'll be safer outside the car!"

Deena and Chuck quickly scrambled out onto the grassy shoulder and away from the pile of cars. Up above, a million stars were sparkling in the sky. Chuck began to trot toward the crowd at the front of the traffic jam. Deena followed him out of curiosity.

"Hey—come back!" her father yelled. Chuck ignored him and kept jogging. Deena hesitated, looked back at her father, then followed Chuck.

At the head of the tangle of cars a red Plymouth sat crumpled against the concrete divider, smoke pouring out of its engine. While Deena and Chuck watched, flames began to lick up from the bottom of the car toward the doors.

"Look out!" someone shouted. "It's on fire!"

The crowd began to move back. Deena watched

with horror as the fire began to grow. She edged back even farther on the shoulder, to get as far away from the car as possible. All at once she noticed that Chuck wasn't with her. He was standing at the front of the crowd, staring at the flames as if he was hypnotized.

Suddenly there was a brokenhearted scream from the crowd. "Tuffy's in there!"

Deena turned to look and saw a young boy holding a bloody towel to his forehead. "Tuffy!" the boy called. "Save Tuffy!"

"There's a dog in the car!" someone else shouted. And now Deena could see the face of a small black and white dog at the back window. The dog was jumping up and down, barking hysterically.

The flames licked higher and higher.

Suddenly someone broke loose from the crowd and began running toward the burning Plymouth.

"No!" shouted a man in the crowd. "It's going to blow up!"

The figure kept running, then disappeared into the thick smoke.

To her horror, Deena realized it was Chuck.

"Chuck! Chuck! Come back!" she shrieked.

But she was too late.

The car exploded in a blazing fireball of red and orange flames.

chapter

3

*E*ven though it was after midnight by the time they got home, and even though school started the next day, Deena couldn't sleep. She just lay in her bed, thinking about everything that had happened that night.

While everyone in the crowd watched in silent horror, Chuck had come running out of the smoke and flames. Mr. Martinson came up just then. "What's going on?" he demanded.

No one answered. They were all staring at Chuck, his face and hands blackened by the explosion, his shirt ripped. He trotted back to the side of the road, carrying the black and white dog in his arms.

"Tuffy! Tuffy!" screamed the little boy.

"Chuck! What in the world?" cried Mr. Martinson.

Chuck ignored everyone for a moment. He was petting the little animal, talking to it soothingly, his blackened face very close to the face of the dog. After a moment he straightened up, then handed the small animal to its owner. "Here, kid," he said.

The boy's mother, who had a big bruise forming on the side of her face, impulsively hugged Chuck. "Oh, thank you," she said. "You don't know how much that dog means to Timmy. You're a hero, you know that?"

"Hey, it's okay," Chuck said, looking embarrassed. "I used to have a dog myself."

Deena gazed at her half-brother with new respect. He was standing there with the goofy grin on his face and he wasn't even hurt, though he'd leapt into a burning car.

Later, lying in bed thinking about it, Deena remembered what the woman had said. To everyone at the accident scene, Chuck *had* been a hero. He must really be brave, she thought.

Or crazy.

The next morning at breakfast Deena decided to let Chuck know she was proud of him and try to make him feel welcome. Her father had already left for work, and her mom was running late as usual.

There wasn't time for anything fancy, so she poured two bowls of bran cereal, then washed a bunch of blueberries and sprinkled them on top. She had almost finished eating hers when Chuck came in, yawning sleepily.

"Hi, Chuck," she said brightly. "I've fixed you some cereal. If we hurry, we can get to school early, and then, if you want, I can introduce you around."

For a moment Chuck just stared at her. "Forget it, kid," he said. "I don't need any help getting along."

"But I only meant—" Deena stopped. Her cheeks were burning as if he had slapped her. He poured some milk on his cereal, not caring if it slopped out onto the table.

A moment or two later Deena's mom came into the kitchen, adjusting an earring. "Hurry up, kids," she said. "I'll drop you at school on the way to the office."

Without a word Chuck stood up and dumped his cereal into the sink. Deena just stared at him. What was the matter with him? she wondered. Was he really crazy?

By the time she got to the lunchroom at noon Deena had nearly forgotten her troubles with Chuck. It was good to be back, she thought. Right after she had filled her tray and found a seat, Rob Morell came sauntering in with a bunch of guys from the track team, trying to look cool the way he always did.

In the past Deena had thought Rob was as cool as he thought he was. After all, he was good-looking, smart, and a star athlete—the kind of boy she could never think of anything to say to. But that day, she felt different. She smiled, remembering her phone call Saturday night, and how she had had Rob eating out of her hand. It gave her a feeling of power, a feeling she could do anything she wanted.

She stared at Rob and smiled, not caring if he saw or not. You might think you're the hottest guy at Shadyside, she thought. But little do you know I'm the girl of your dreams. Yes, me. Shy, quiet little Deena!

"Yoo-hoo! Anybody home?"

Deena looked up, startled out of her daydream of power over Rob. Jade was standing behind her, holding a lunch tray. She was wearing a yellow- and white-striped sundress, and her long red hair was tied back with a white ribbon. She looked fabulous. In fact, all the boys in the lunchroom were staring at her.

"Well? Do want me to join you? Or are you going to spend the rest of the afternoon in the clouds?"

"Sure, Jade, have a seat," Deena said.

Jade set her tray down, then sat next to her friend. "I thought you'd be eating with your new brother," she said.

Deena shrugged. "He's made it pretty clear he's not interested in socializing with his little sister," she said. She tried to sound as if she didn't care one way or the other.

"Oh," said Jade, looking disappointed. Then she brightened and began looking around the crowded lunchroom. "Well, what does he look like, at least? Where is he?"

"He's—" Deena swiveled her head around the lunchroom, but she saw no sign of Chuck. "Well, I don't know where he is," she said. She frowned, suddenly nervous. Why wasn't Chuck at lunch? she wondered. She knew they had the same lunch period.

"I'll meet him some other time," Jade said. Then she leaned forward. "Guess who's just become the hot couple of the month?" she said.

"Who?" said Deena.

"Bruce Kipness and Sherry Murdoch!"

"Really?" Deena said. Bruce and Sherry were the two fattest kids in the school.

"They're both in my geography class, and they walked in holding hands this morning," said Jade.

"Well, I guess that's nice," said Deena.

"Yeah, probably no one else would want to go out with either of them," said Jade. "Oh, and I've got to tell you what Mrs. Overton was wearing. You know she cut her hair really short—almost as short as a boy's."

"What?" said Deena.

"I said Mrs. Overton—what's the matter with you?" said Jade, sounding exasperated.

"I don't know," Deena said. "I guess I'm a little worried about Chuck. Somehow I have a feeling he—"

Before she could finish her thought, her words were cut off by a sudden banging as the cafeteria doors flew open. Deena turned to look, but all she could see were two bodies crashing into a stack of used trays by the door.

"Fight!" someone shouted, and the room echoed with the noise of chairs being scraped back, dishes and silverware clattering onto the tables.

By now everyone was standing, and a crowd had started to gather by the doors. Deena was on tiptoe, struggling to see who it was.

"It's Bobby McCorey," Jade called over the excited shouts of the other kids. "He's fighting with some new kid!"

Uh-oh, Deena thought. She climbed up on the chair to see. "Oh, no," she groaned. "It's Chuck."

"Look out!" a girl beside her cried. "The new kid's got a knife!"

chapter
4

*O*kay, okay.

So he was having a little trouble keeping it together. Big deal.

The plan was still working, right on schedule. Still no one suspected a thing.

Only one more week now. One more week and he could put the final step of his plan into effect.

One more week and all his troubles would be over.

Nothing could stop him now. Nothing and nobody.

It would just be too bad for anyone who tried.

chapter
5

*T*his school year was going to be a disaster. Deena was sure of it. It was Saturday afternoon, the kind of late summer day when you knew fall would be coming soon. She was standing in the circular driveway in front of her house wearing an old bathing suit under cutoff shorts, washing her mother's silver-colored Civic.

But her mind wasn't on the Honda, it was on all the awful things that had happened the past week.

First there were her classes—all of them were harder than she'd expected. Why had she decided to take trigonometry? She'd never pass it in a million years.

Second was her social life. It was going to be a replay of last year, when the only reason she ever got asked to parties was because she was Jade's friend. She felt even more tongue-tied this year than last, if that was possible.

And last, but definitely not least, was the biggest problem of all. Her brother Chuck.

She still had trouble believing that he'd been stupid enough to get into a fight the first day of school. Even worse, he'd been carrying a knife. It took three teachers to break it up. What a temper Chuck had! The only reason he hadn't been kicked out was that her father had gone to the principal and practically guaranteed there would be no more trouble.

Deena had overheard her father yelling at Chuck the night after it happened. "And another thing!" Mr. Martinson had shouted in a voice Deena had only heard once or twice before. "If you make so much as one misstep—even being caught without a hall pass—you'll be kicked out on your ear! Do you understand?"

Deena couldn't hear Chuck's answer, but she could imagine the look on his face—the *snowl*.

That was practically the only expression she'd seen on his face all week. He was grounded indefinitely, but instead of trying to make the best of things and hanging out with the family he disappeared into his room in the basement right after school and stayed there the whole evening, emerging only to eat a silent dinner.

It was almost as if he wasn't there. Deena wouldn't have minded, except the whole atmosphere of the house had changed. Everyone was on edge. Deena's father, who was usually the most easygoing man in the world, had become short-tempered, snapping at Deena and her mother over nothing. And Deena's mom, who was always tense anyway because of her job as chief administrator at the Shadyside Social Services Agency, had become even more jumpy than usual.

Deena sighed. Who said your teen years were the best of your life? she wondered. She watched as the soapy water slid down the gleaming sides of the Civic, then turned on the hose and began to spray the car down.

"Hey, Deena!" She looked up to see Jade walking up the long flagstone path to the driveway.

"Hi, Jade," said Deena. "What's doing?"

Jade shrugged. She was wearing a tight, sleeveless white knit shirt and green shorts, and her hair shimmered like liquid copper in the late-afternoon sunlight. "I was supposed to go out with Mike Kamiskey tonight," she said, "but he just called to cancel. He has a bad cold—or so he says—so I thought I'd come over and see what you're up to."

"You knew I wouldn't have a date, you mean," said Deena.

"Hey, don't get all uptight," said Jade. "I just thought I'd drop by is all."

Deena turned off the hose and stood looking at the car critically. "Hey, it's okay," she said. "My mom and dad went into the city for a concert. They left me money to order in pizza and rent a couple of movies. You're welcome to join me."

"Sounds like fun," said Jade. Then she smiled her mischievous smile. "What about Chuck?" she asked.

"Forget about him," said Deena. "He's Mr. Antisocial. He only comes out of his room to eat."

"I'll bet I could change that," Jade said.

"I said forget it!"

"Okay, okay," said Jade. "He sure is good-looking. What a waste!"

* * *

"I don't believe I washed the car," Deena said, staring out the window. It had been pouring rain for the last hour.

"My mother says it never fails," said Jade. "Washing the car can make it rain even if there aren't any clouds in the sky."

"Want more pizza?" Deena asked after a moment. She pushed the big square box across the coffee table to her friend.

"I'm stuffed," said Jade. "Maybe we ought to see if Chuck wants some."

"Will you forget about him?" said Deena. "He's probably in his room plotting to overthrow the whole high school. Come on, let's watch another tape."

"I have a better idea," Jade said. "I think it's time for Rob Morell to get another call—from his secret admirer."

"Oh, Jade, I don't know," said Deena. For some reason her heart had started beating fast, as if she had just run a race.

"Come on, Deena," pleaded Jade. "Let your secret side out."

"Well, I suppose it's just harmless fun," said Deena.

"Exactly," said Jade. "Harmless, and fun." She already had the phone book open and was punching the numbers into Deena's phone. She held the phone to her ear a moment, then thrust it into Deena's hand. "Here!" she said, sounding excited.

It was just like last week, only better. Deena wasn't the least bit nervous once she started talking. If anyone was nervous, it was Rob! He was tripping all over his tongue.

"Well, couldn't we go out for a cuff of coppee?" he asked her after a few minutes of chatting.

"I think you mean *cup* of *coffee,* Rob," Deena said in her sexy whisper. "And I'd like that a lot. But first I have to be sure—"

"Sure of what?"

"Of you, and of things." She was trying to think of more to say when there was a sudden, hollow click on the line.

"Hello?" said Rob. "Hello, are you still there?" He sounded afraid that she had hung up.

"There must be trouble on the line," said Deena. "I'm sorry, Rob, but I have to go now. I'll call again one evening soon." She hung up, feeling giddy with power.

"That was great!" said Jade. "But what was that noise?"

"I don't know," said Deena. "Maybe there's something wrong with the phone."

"I hope not," Jade said. "Hand it over. It's my turn."

"Who are you going to call?"

"I thought I'd try Mike Kamiskey," she said. "Find out if he *really* had a cold tonight." She began punching in the numbers, but before she could finish there were three hard knocks on the door, and it swung open. There stood Chuck, wearing cutoffs and a turquoise-colored R.E.M. T-shirt, grinning in that goofy way he had. "Hello, girls," he said.

"Chuck, didn't you ever hear of privacy?" said Deena.

"Hey—we're family, right?" countered Chuck.

Then, turning to Jade, he added, "What's *your* name?"

Deena glanced at Jade. She was looking at Chuck as if he were the lead singer in the world's hottest new rock band. Deena sighed. "Chuck," she said, "this is—"

"I'm Jade Smith," cut in Jade, smiling her widest, most honey-dripping smile.

"I'm Chuck," said Chuck, smiling right back.

And I'm going to throw up, Deena thought.

Chuck sat on the antique bench Deena kept in front of her dressing table. With his powerful muscles and big frame he made it look like a piece of doll furniture.

"What are you doing in here?" said Deena.

"Hanging out," said Chuck. "But I don't need to ask what you girls are doing in here. Or should I say— what you're up to."

"What do you mean?" said Deena.

" 'This is your secret admirer, Rob,' " he said in an imitation of Deena's sexy whisper. " 'I'd just love to get together with you sometime. . . .' "

"You've been spying on us!" said Deena. She felt herself blush to the roots of her hair.

"That explains the clicking noise," said Jade.

"I wasn't spying," said Chuck. "I just happened to pick up the phone. I'm sure Dad would be interested in what you're up to."

"Chuck, no!" said Deena. "You wouldn't tell! Dad would take my phone away!"

"So what?" said Chuck. "You don't need one if all you know how to do is make silly calls to a bunch of stupid high school boys. I mean, if you want to play around on the phone, at least have some imagination."

"And I suppose you have a better idea?"

"I might," said Chuck.

"Stop arguing, you two," said Jade, not looking at all perturbed. She gave Chuck a mischievous smile. "Why don't you show us what you have in mind?"

"Wait a minute," said Deena. "Why don't we just forget the whole thing? I don't think—"

"Come on, Deena," said Jade. "It's just harmless fun. You said so yourself. What's wrong with letting Chuck in on it, too?"

Oh, no, thought Deena. Chuck's ideas were bound to be trouble, but what could she do? If Chuck told on her, that would be the end of her telephone, if not of her entire social life. And after all, Chuck was acting sort of friendly right then. Maybe he was just lonely.

"Okay," Chuck said, "but no more of this dinky 'Oh, Rob, you're so handsome' stuff. Let's make some real calls."

"Like what?" said Jade.

"Let me see the phone book," said Chuck. He thumbed through the Shadyside directory for a moment. "What a hick town," he mumbled. "What do people do around here for fun?" he asked after a minute.

"A million things," said Deena, feeling furious. "The same things you do in the city, probably. Go to movies, go dancing, miniature golfing, bowling. . . ."

"Bowling, that's good," said Chuck. He flipped through the yellow pages. "Here we go—Shadyside Lanes." He punched in a number. After a moment a woman's voice sounded over the speaker phone.

"Good evening, Shadyside Lanes."

"I'm only going to tell you once," said Chuck. He

had dropped his voice really low and was speaking in a kind of gravelly tone. "There's a bomb planted somewhere on your premises. It's timed to go off at ten."

"Who is this?" demanded the woman. She sounded scared.

"You have fifteen minutes to evacuate," said Chuck. And he hung up the phone.

"Chuck!" said Deena, shocked and appalled. "How could you do that? Calling in a bomb threat is serious!"

"Hey, it's probably the only exciting thing that's happened around here in months," said Chuck. He laughed and began flipping through the phone book again.

"It is sort of a funny idea," said Jade. "I mean, all those people standing out in the rain in their bowling shoes."

"Jade!" said Deena. "For heaven's sake! It's a crime to make bomb threats!"

"You're right," said Jade. "Chuck," she said, her voice all honey again, "we were just calling kids from the school. I mean, we don't want to get in trouble."

"Yeah, yeah, yeah," said Chuck. Then he snapped his fingers. "Wait a minute, I've got an idea. What's the name of that place that's supposed to be so spooky?"

"You mean Fear Street?" said Deena.

"Yeah, that's it. What a name!" Chuck laughed again.

"It's named after some creepy old guy named Simon Fear," Deena told him. "You'd better not make fun of it," she added. "Terrible things have happened on Fear Street. Really."

"Like what?" said Chuck, grinning.

"People have disappeared," said Jade. "And there have been a number of unsolved murders. Late at night people have heard weird screams from the Fear Street woods."

Chuck looked at her with the goofy grin on his face. "Get real," he said. "Don't you know that every small town has some place like Fear Street? It's all a bunch of garbage just to make a boring place a little more interesting."

"Fear Street is real, Chuck," said Deena.

"It's not something to fool around with," Jade added. Deena noticed that Jade was deadly serious, for once not flirting.

"Real or not," said Chuck, "I'm not afraid of Fear Street. Let's see, now," he said, continuing to flip through the phone book. "You want to call kids from school, right?" he said. "What's the name of that kid that picked a fight with me the other day?"

"Bobby McCorey," said Jade immediately. "He and his buddies think they're hot stuff. They're always pushing the little guys around."

"Well, let's try pushing him for a change," said Chuck. "See how tough he really is." Before Deena could talk him out of it, Chuck had called Bobby's number.

"May I speak to Bobby McCorey?" he said in the weird, gravelly voice. Deena felt a chill go up her back. After a moment Bobby's voice came on.

"This is Bobby," he said.

"This is the Phantom of Fear Street," said Chuck. "And I've got my eye on you."

"The Phantom of—who is this?" said Bobby.

"I've got my eye on you," Chuck repeated.

"What do you mean?" All of a sudden Bobby didn't sound so confident.

"Just what I said," said Chuck. "I've got my eye on you—the evil eye. If I were you, I'd make sure all the doors and windows are locked tonight—and every night."

"Say, who is this?" said Bobby, his voice shaky. Deena was about to grab the phone from Chuck when he gave a maniacal cackle and hung up the phone.

"You're right, Jade," said Chuck. "It's much more fun to call up the kids from school."

"I don't believe you did that!" cried Deena. "Bobby McCorey is really a bad guy. What if he recognized your voice?"

"Don't sweat it," said Chuck. "It's just harmless fun. Or maybe *you're* afraid of the Phantom of Fear Street!" He laughed, then ran to the window and raised it. Outside it was raining harder than ever, and the sky rippled with lightning.

"Spirits of Fear Street!" Chuck yelled at the top of his voice. "Do you hear me? I'm waiting for you! Right here! Come and get me!"

He's crazy, Deena thought. He gets that wild look on his face, and his whole personality changes. It's like he's two people, and the side of him that loves danger can take over in an instant.

Suddenly there was a terrific flash of lightning and at the same time a rolling clap of thunder. In the next instant the lights went out, and the total darkness was pierced only by a bloodcurdling scream.

After a moment the lights flickered on, and the two girls gaped at each other with wide eyes.

"That lightning was close!" said Deena in a shaky voice. "It might have even struck—"

"Deena!" cried Jade urgently. "Where's Chuck?"

Deena took in the room—but Chuck was nowhere! Then there was a groan over by the window.

"Over here," said Jade. "Quick!"

The girls ran over to the still-open window. Rain slanted in, and another flash of lightning illuminated Chuck, his limp body curled up on the floor.

chapter

6

For a moment Deena just stared at the still form of her brother. "Chuck!" she screamed. "Chuck!"

"Oh, no!" cried Jade, her voice trembling. She bent over him. "What do you think—is he—is he—AARGH!"

Jade and Deena both jumped back at the same moment as Chuck sat up, screaming, "Booga, booga!" Then he lay down on the floor again, laughing so hard he started to choke.

"I sure had you going there," he gasped between laughs and coughs. "Guess the so-called spirits of Fear Street had you girls scared half to death!"

Deena had never felt so many intense emotions so quickly in her life. First had been fright—terrible fright. Then shock, then relief when she realized Chuck was all right. But what she felt now, the strongest of all, was anger. Anger that filled her body until she thought she would explode.

"Chuck, you stupid creep!" she shouted. "That was really the pits! You shouldn't go messing around with things you don't understand!"

"I'm s-s-sorry," Chuck said, breathless from laughter. But he didn't sound sorry. "But, hey—I just couldn't resist."

All the excitement of the last hour gone, Jade pressed close to the window to glance out. "The rain's letting up," she said. "I guess I'll go on home."

"If you don't mind, I'll walk you," said Chuck. "After all, there are strange—*things* out there in the night." And he started laughing again, turning his goofy grin on Jade. Deena was still furious, but Jade didn't seem to mind at all. In fact, she was looking at Chuck as if she didn't care if he *was* the Phantom of Fear Street.

The next day Chuck apologized and offered to help Deena with her math homework. It was as if he were two people, she thought. One Chuck—the one with the grin—was kind, and brave, and funny. The other Chuck was mean and immature. Deena was beginning to care a lot for the first Chuck. She just had to think of a way to encourage that side of him.

She was still thinking about the two Chucks the next day at school and nearly bumped into Rob Morell in the hall on her way to French class. "Excuse me," she said.

"My fault," said Rob. "How you doing, Deena?" He gave her a big, friendly smile, and her heart began to pound as she stammered an answer. She remembered the past week, when she had felt so powerful after her first anonymous call to Rob.

But after what happened the past Saturday night she didn't feel powerful anymore. Instead she felt a little dirty and ashamed. She wasn't sure what had changed, except that the calls Chuck had made were mean. They could even be dangerous. The calling game wasn't fun anymore.

And she wasn't going to do it again. She'd talk to Jade and Chuck and convince them to stop.

She had her chance in the lunchroom later that morning. She was just about to bite into her mystery-meat sandwich when Jade plopped her tray down across the table. "Deena, did you see this morning's paper?" she asked, her eyes sparkling with mischief.

"No," Deena admitted. "Listen, Jade, I've got to talk to you—"

"Sure," said Jade. "But first take a look at this!" She thrust the Shadyside *Morning Press* at Deena, nearly knocking over Deena's milk carton. It was open to the front page, and an article was circled in red. As Deena began to read she felt her heart sink.

BOMB THREAT A HOAX, POLICE SAY

Shadyside police were called to investigate a bomb threat at the Shadyside Lanes at 9:45 P.M. Saturday night. Although the entire building was evacuated, officers found no trace of explosives.

Louise Cameron, night manager for Shadyside Lanes, reported that the phoned threat was made by a male with a hoarse voice. "He sounded like he meant business," she said.

Cory Brooks, a student at Shadyside High School, was among the more than thirty patrons who waited outside in the rain while the building was searched. "Nobody panicked," he said. "But I wish they'd have let me finish my game. I was bowling the best game of my life."

Although they admit they have no leads, police spokesman Lt. Evan Frazier says the investigation is continuing. "It may have been just a crank call," he told the *Press*. "But we can't rule out terrorism. We're taking this threat very seriously."

When she had finished reading the article Deena felt sick and ashamed. She glanced over at Jade, expecting to see shame on her face. Instead, Jade's eyes were shining, and her face was flushed. She looked excited. "Can you *believe* it?" she said. "We actually made the front page of the paper!"

For a moment Deena just stared at her friend in disbelief. "Are you crazy?" she said. "This is serious. It says here that the police are investigating."

"Oh, they'll never find us," said Jade.

"What's this 'us' stuff, anyway?" Deena went on. "It was Chuck who phoned in the bomb threat."

"Lighten up," said Jade. "Nobody was hurt."

"No," Deena agreed, "but they could have been. What if someone had panicked at the bowling alley? And what about that other call—the one Chuck made pretending to be the Phantom of Fear Street?"

For a moment Jade's face changed, and Deena could see a flicker of fear in her eyes. "What about it?" Jade finally said.

"That wasn't so harmless," Deena went on. "That call was really scary. He really wanted to frighten Bobby McCorey."

Jade was frowning now. "All right—so maybe Chuck shouldn't mess around with Fear Street when he makes calls. But I like telephoning, and you do, too. Admit it, Deena."

"Well, maybe the calls we made to kids at school were fun," said Deena, "but Chuck's already in enough trouble. And I don't trust him. Besides, making those calls is basically wrong. We've got to stop."

"Oh, really?" snapped Jade. "Since when are you a majority? It seems to me there are three of us involved. Maybe Chuck and I ought to have a say."

"It's my phone," said Deena.

"Well, then," said Jade, "maybe I ought to tell Rob Morell who's been calling him on *her phone*." She stopped and smiled nastily at Deena's sudden look of horror. "Or," Jade went on, "we can wait for Saturday night, and the three of us can discuss it together."

By Saturday night Deena was more convinced than ever that she had made the right decision. Making those phone calls was wrong, and she was going to put a stop to them no matter what. Besides, she didn't think Chuck would really tell her father what they'd been up to. After all, he was involved, too. Jade couldn't possibly tell Rob Morell—could she? She'd just gotten a little carried away by the excitement, that was all.

On the bright side, Deena was getting along with Chuck much better. He had helped her twice during the week with her trig homework and even loaded the dishwasher one night. Maybe Jade was right. He was just lonely. Maybe he was finally adjusting to life in Shadyside.

That night Deena's parents went to visit friends, as they usually did on Saturdays. Deena had decided that a barbecue might be the best thing to put Chuck and Jade in a mellow mood for their discussion. It was a perfect night for a cookout. She made hamburger patties with pieces of cheese inside and her special potato salad with onion, tomatoes, and sliced black olives.

While Chuck got the fire going Deena finished setting the redwood table outside. There was a knock on the gate, and Jade came in carrying a big tub of ice cream.

"Smells delish," Jade said. She was wearing one of her jumpsuits, this one made of faded denim and covered with fake patches in bright colors. Deena saw Chuck look at her appreciatively before he turned back to the barbecue.

The hamburgers were perfect, charred outside and juicy on the inside, and both Jade and Chuck had seconds and thirds of the potato salad. After the meal Chuck seemed to relax for the first time since he had come to Shadyside.

Maybe everything was going to be all right after all, Deena thought. The three teens were sitting on the patio in lounge chairs, eating peach ice cream and listening to Deena's portable tape player. The sky had darkened to the deep purple that comes before true night, and Deena had her head tilted back, watching the stars appear one by one.

"Great dinner, Deena," said Chuck, and she

smiled. He had actually called her by her name instead of "kid."

"I love that salad," said Jade. "The whole thing was fabulous."

Okay, Deena told herself. There will never be a better moment. "Listen, guys," she said. "We have to have a serious talk. I don't think we should make any more of those phone calls."

"Okay," said Chuck.

"Fine," said Jade.

"In fact," Deena went on, "I think we—" She stopped. "*What* did you say?" she asked.

"We agree," said Jade. "Chuck and I already talked it over."

"Yeah," Chuck said. "Jade convinced me it's dumb to take a chance like that. Especially since our old man works for the phone company."

Deena turned to stare at her brother and her friend. Jade had convinced him? When had they talked? It looked as if Jade was going to be a good influence on Chuck whether he liked it or not!

"What else did you want to talk about?" asked Jade.

"Nothing—I guess," said Deena. She had never expected to win so easily.

It was almost completely dark now, but she saw Chuck's hand slide across the space between his chair and Jade's to clasp Jade's hand. Deena felt a flash of jealousy for a moment and thought of Rob Morell, but mostly she was glad for Jade and Chuck. It looked as if they could be good for each other.

Deena was thinking that it was so peaceful and nice out there that she could stay forever, eating ice cream and hanging out. The last strains of Dire Straits died down, and she got up to change the tape. She was just pushing the eject button when a dark, fluttering shape brushed her face. She screamed and jumped back.

"What's wrong?" called Chuck.

"There's a—a bat!" Deena cried in horror. She ducked and ran into the den through the sliding door. Outside the bat was fluttering crazily around the patio light.

"A *bat?*" Jade shrieked. She jumped up and followed Deena inside.

"Hey, girls," said Chuck. "Relax. It's not carrying a switchblade or anything."

"Very funny," called Deena from inside. "Bats give me the creeps!"

"Me, too," said Jade. "Chuck, come on *in*."

"Sure," he said. He slid the door open and stood for a moment in the opening.

"Close it!" shrieked both Jade and Deena. "*Close* it! You'll let the bat in!"

"Here, bat, bat, bat," Chuck said. But he slid the door shut and flopped into the leather armchair by the fireplace. "What is it with you two?" he said. "Are small-town girls afraid of everything?"

"Most people with any sense are afraid of bats," said Deena. "They can carry rabies."

"That's not why you're afraid of them," said Chuck. "It's superstition. Just like that nonsense about Fear Street."

"Fear Street *isn't* nonsense," said Jade. She sat down on the arm of the chair next to Chuck. Deena thought she looked beautiful in the dim light, and also afraid.

40

"Don't you see?" said Chuck. "All that stuff you've heard happened on Fear Street—it's all exaggerated or made up. It's like the boogeyman. People tell those stories to scare each other."

"For your information," said Deena, "there are no birds in the Fear Street woods. Scientists from all over the country haven't been able to find out why."

Chuck laughed. "No birds," he said. "Now that's what I call a terrifying problem."

"People have disappeared," said Jade. "Houses have mysteriously burned down—"

"Ha!" said Chuck. "Houses. You mean people actually live on Fear Street?"

"Well, yes," Deena said.

"Who, then?" said Chuck. "Monsters, ogres, witches, Dracula?"

"I don't know," said Deena. The conversation was making her more and more nervous. "I don't know anyone who lives there."

"That's just the point," said Chuck. "Now I'm going to prove to you that there's nothing about Fear Street to be scared of. I'll show you that only ordinary people live there." He switched on the overhead light and reached for the phone book.

"Chuck, what are you doing?" cried Deena. "You promised—"

"I promised not to make any more prank phone calls," said Chuck. "This is different—I'm about to change your lives forever. After this you'll never be afraid again."

His finger had stopped at a number in the book, and he reached for the phone.

"Who are you calling?" asked Jade. Her face was

glowing with excitement the way it had the weekend before.

"I don't know," said Chuck. "It's just the first name I found listed on Fear Street." He switched on the loudspeaker and punched in the number. The burring sound of the phone on Fear Street filled the room. "I'm going to prove to both of you that there's nothing to be afraid of."

The phone kept ringing. Deena counted fifteen before Chuck said, "No one home, I guess. I'll have to find another—"

On the sixteenth ring there was a click, followed immediately by a breathless gasp. Then the shrillest, most frightened-sounding voice Deena had ever heard cried out: "Please! Please come quickly! He's going to kill me!"

chapter
7

"Who is this?" demanded Chuck.

"Please," the woman begged. "Whoever you are, you're my only hope! Any minute now he'll—" But her voice was cut off by a man's bellow of rage. While the three teens listened, horrified, the speaker phone amplified terror-stricken screams and then the sound of shattering glass.

"Hello? Hello?" Chuck said into the phone.

And then the woman was back. "Please come!" she begged again. "Please help me! You're my only—" There was the sound of a slap, and then a new, gruff voice came on the line.

"Who is this?" the voice growled.

"What's going on there?" countered Chuck.

"It's none of your business," growled the man. "You've got the wrong number, do you understand?"

"But I heard—" Chuck began.

"The wrong number!" the man repeated, and he hung up the phone.

Deena, Chuck, and Jade just looked at one another. Finally Jade broke the silence, her voice soft and scared sounding. "That was another trick call, Chuck, right?" she said.

Deena had been thinking—or hoping—the same thing. But when she saw Chuck's pale face she knew it hadn't been a joke.

"It was real," he said. "Unless someone's playing a trick on *me*." He looked grim and angry.

"Oh, no," said Deena, her legs suddenly weak. "What are we going to do?"

"We've got to call the police," said Jade, reaching for the phone.

"Wait," said Chuck, grabbing her wrist. "How are we going to explain how I happened to make the call? And why should they believe us? They'll think we're just kids pulling phone pranks."

"Like that bomb threat," whispered Jade.

"Exactly," said Chuck.

"We ought to tell *someone*," said Deena. "That woman sounded like she was in terrible trouble. She said he was—he was going to kill her!"

"Maybe they were just playing a party game," said Jade, but she didn't sound as if she believed it.

"That was no game," said Deena. She stood up. "If neither of you will do it, then I'm going to call—"

Chuck snatched the phone off the table. "Will you cool it?" he said. He reached for the phone book.

"The police emergency number is nine-one-one," Deena told him.

"I'm not calling the police," Chuck said. "I'm

getting the address." He shut the book with a snap and stood up.

"You mean you're going over there?" cried Deena, horrified.

"I've got to," said Chuck. "I've got to find out what's going on."

"Let the authorities find out," said Deena. "What if there's really a maniac loose?"

"Then I've got to stop him," Chuck said. "You heard her. I'm her only hope."

"I'm going, too," said Jade. She began to pull on her flannel jacket. "You can't go over there alone, Chuck."

Deena took a deep breath. "I think you're both crazy," she said. "Maybe I am, too. I'll drive. Chuck doesn't know his way around Shadyside yet." She got her mother's extra car keys from the hook at the bottom of the kitchen bulletin board, then followed the others outside.

It was a clear, chilly night with a large crescent moon. Deena slid in behind the wheel, Chuck in the bucket seat next to her, Jade in the back.

"What's the address?" Deena asked, taking the car around the long circular driveway.

"Eight eighty-four Fear Street," said Chuck. "The people's name is Farberson."

"Eight eighty-four!" said Jade. "That must be out near the cemetery."

Deena shivered. She had never been to Fear Street at night and, like most people who lived in Shadyside, tried to avoid it during the day. She turned on Division Street, which divided Shadyside into north and south halves, then south on Mill Road, knowing Fear Street would be coming up soon. Although street lamps illuminated the road and the woods to the side, Deena kept seeing things move in the shadows.

Chuck and Jade must have felt the same way she did, because nobody said a word until she turned onto Fear Street.

At first glance it could have been any other street, with its old houses and empty yards. But on closer inspection there was something different about Fear Street.

For one thing, there were the ruins of old Simon Fear's mansion, which had burned down long ago—but was still rumored to be haunted.

For another thing, the shadows on Fear Street were thicker and darker than those anywhere else in town. And most of all, there was a feeling of death, of lifelessness. The lawns were more brown than green, and the scraggly trees had only a few moth-eaten leaves on them. Though lights burned in a few of the windows of the houses on both sides of Fear Street, there was no feeling of warmth, of happy family life behind the curtains.

"What was that address again?" Deena said. She hoped her voice didn't sound as scared as she felt.

"Eight eighty-four," said Chuck.

"Three fifty, four twenty-two," read Jade from signs on the mailboxes. "Keep going."

Deena guided the Civic deeper and deeper down Fear Street. She usually loved to drive her mom's little car, but that night she wished it was something bigger and more powerful—like maybe a tank!

Looming dead ahead in the darkness was the black shape of Fear Street woods. There were only a few houses left now, and Deena began to hope that Chuck had been wrong about the address. That it wasn't 884 Fear Street, or even Fear Street at all, but Hawthorne, or Mill Road, or Canyon Drive, or—

"Up there, that's it!" said Chuck.

Just ahead of them was one more house, set apart from the neighboring houses, a two-story Victorian with battered shingles and a patchy lawn. Beyond it was nothing—but the cemetery.

Deena's headlights picked out "884" on a rusty mailbox. She parked in front of the house and cut the lights.

The three teens looked at the house for a moment. It was in total darkness. In fact, it looked as if it had been completely deserted for years!

"There's no one home, Chuck," said Deena. "You must have copied the wrong address."

"Maybe," said Chuck uncertainly. "But I've got to check."

"I think Deena's right, Chuck," said Jade, sounding very nervous. "This must be the wrong place."

"I'm just going to look around," said Chuck. "You girls wait here." He opened the car door and started to get out.

Deena remembered how fearlessly he had run to the burning car to rescue the dog. She knew he wasn't about to be talked out of his plan. "There's a flashlight in the glove compartment," she said.

"Thanks," he replied. He took out the flashlight, then, in the light from the ceiling bulb, he flashed his goofy grin for a moment. He shut the door and began the walk up the crumbling driveway.

Deena and Jade sat silent in the darkness. Deena

thought briefly of locking all the car doors but then decided Chuck might have to get back in in a hurry.

Across the street she could just make out the dark, looming shapes of trees in the Fear Street woods. On the far side of the house was the outline of the stone wall around the cemetery. From behind it there was a faint, eerie glow from the moon.

"I don't know about you, but I'm not staying here another second!" said Jade suddenly. "I'm going with Chuck."

"Wait for me," said Deena. The two girls scrambled out of the car and started up the driveway after Chuck. As Deena felt the gravel crunch underfoot she imagined it was broken bones and felt a shiver go through her.

They found Chuck standing on the porch, his ear to the door. "I rang the bell," he said. "I can't hear anything." He knocked, tentatively at first, then louder.

"The curtains are all drawn," he said. "Let's go see if there's anything around back."

The girls followed him off the porch and around the side of the house. Something soft and sticky brushed against Deena's face, and she stifled a scream. As she brushed it away she realized it was only a cobweb— then she began to wonder what sort of spider had made that huge web.

The shutters were closed all along the side of the house. But when they got to the back door Chuck suddenly raised his hand. "Whoa!" he whispered.

The glass in the top half of the back door was broken, and the door itself was hanging slightly ajar. With Jade and Deena crowded in behind him, Chuck

shone the flashlight through the broken window, re-
vealing an old-fashioned kitchen. In the center of the
room a table lay on its side. All around, the floor was
littered with broken dishes. Chuck swung the flashlight
to the counter, where canisters and jars lay smashed,
their contents of flour, sugar, and spices spilled over
the counter and onto the floor.

Chuck let out a low whistle. "The place has been
ransacked," he said. "I'm going in." As he swung the
door open the rest of the way, it creaked on its hinges
like the cry of some creature long dead.

Deena's heart was pounding so loudly she was sure
the others could hear it. Holding her breath, she
followed Chuck and Jade into the kitchen. Chuck
continued to inch forward, aiming the flashlight just
ahead of him. Then he stopped so suddenly Deena and
Jade nearly walked into him.

Just beyond the door to the living room, illuminated
by his circle of light, lay an outstretched arm. Next to
its hand was a telephone receiver. Splattered over both
were bright drops of red blood, running and collecting
into a dark, spreading pool on the carpet.

chapter

8

*F*or a moment nobody moved. Then Chuck began to walk toward the scene of horror, shining the flashlight ahead of him. "Stay back!" he warned the girls. He bent down, then stood up again quickly.

"It's a woman," he said in a shaky voice. "I think she's been stabbed."

"Stabbed?" shrieked Jade.

"Go back to the car!" he said. "She must have surprised whoever broke into the place. He might still be here!"

Deena had never been so scared in her life. Her legs turned to overcooked spaghetti. "Come on," she whispered. "Jade—Chuck—let's get out of here!"

"You two go on," Chuck said. "I've got to find a phone."

"Let's call from somewhere else," said Jade.

"There may not be time!" said Chuck. "This woman needs an ambulance!" He reached over to the wall and flicked on a switch. The sudden brightness was startling, and Deena had to blink several times before she could see. She stepped gingerly into the living room with Jade and suddenly felt faint. The woman was lying on her stomach. Beside her on the floor lay a big, blood-covered carving knife.

"Oh, nooo," said Jade, her voice a faint moan. Involuntarily she clutched Deena's hand.

Deena glanced around the living room to avoid staring at the woman. The room looked as if a storm had blown through it. Lamps and ashtrays lay broken on the floor. The couch was slit open, its stuffing spilling out. Pictures were pulled from the walls and lay smashed with the other debris.

Chuck was bent over one of the few standing tables, dialing the phone. "Hello," he said. "I want to report a—"

Before he could finish he heard loud footsteps on the stairway to his left.

"Someone else is here!" Jade cried.

A large, heavy man dressed in a green overcoat and wearing a black ski mask appeared on the stairway. In his right hand he held a tire iron. "What are you doing here?" he growled in a deep, hollow voice.

"You stabbed her!" said Chuck. "You broke in and stabbed her! You'll never get away with it!"

"Drop the phone," the man said, chilling menace in his voice. He hurried down the last few stairs, the tire iron in front of him, and, as Jade and Deena watched in horror, began to advance on Chuck.

"Chuck!" screamed Deena. "Look out!"

Chuck jumped to the side just as the tire iron came swinging down, narrowly missing his head. His eyes darted wildly around the living room, then came to rest where the woman lay. He lunged forward, the masked man after him. Chuck quickly snatched up the carving knife and held it in front of him menacingly. "Back off, mister!" he said.

The stranger stopped a moment, then nodded slowly. "You won't use that knife," he said. "Better put it down."

"Run, girls!" cried Chuck.

Quickly Deena and Jade ran past the masked man and out the front door. Chuck kept the heavy, bloodspattered blade of the knife pointed at the intruder.

"Put down the knife," the man repeated in his deep voice. "You'll never use it." He reached out one gloved hand as if to take the knife from Chuck.

Chuck bounded toward the front door. When he reached it he heaved the knife at the masked man. It hit the wall over the intruder's head and bounced to the floor.

Chuck burst out the door, and then all three of them were running—running for their lives.

"Quick, get in!" shouted Chuck. He shoved the girls into the backseat of the car, then ran around and slid into the driver's seat.

"Deena, the keys!" he shouted.

Deena frantically began to search through her jacket pockets. In the moonlight they could see the masked man stumbling down the driveway. He was heading straight for them when she remembered. "They're still in the ignition!"

Chuck flipped on the motor and floored the accelerator. With a squeal the car spun away from the curb. Chuck gunned it to the end of the street—a dead end.

"Chuck!" cried Jade. "He's getting into his car! Hurry!"

Deena turned and saw the man get into an old-model sedan in the driveway of the house. Chuck slammed the Civic into reverse. "Hold on!" he shouted. He gunned the car backward along the way they had come. The stranger pulled out of the driveway and was coming after them.

Chuck continued to floor the pedal, flying backward past the dark houses all along Fear Street and out onto the Mill Road. Too late, Deena saw the lights of a big truck bearing down on them from the south. "Look out!" she shouted.

Chuck wrenched the steering wheel, and the Honda fishtailed onto the shoulder. The truck swerved past, just missing them, its horn blaring. The little car was still skidding.

"Look out! We're going into a ditch!" Deena screamed.

But somehow Chuck managed to get control. Breathing a sigh of relief, he spun the car around and began speeding north on the Mill Road.

"He's still following us!" shrieked Jade. "Faster!"

"Which way?" shouted Chuck.

"Turn left!" cried Deena. With a protesting squeal the little car turned onto Canyon Drive. The masked man's headlights were still behind them. "Turn right!" Deena screamed. "Now left!"

The little car swerved so hard that Deena thought it might fall apart. They hit a deep hole in the road, and Deena's head hit the roof. Before she could regain her balance Chuck had swerved again, and then again onto a narrow dirt road.

"Have we lost him?" Jade cried, sounding weak.

"I think so," Chuck replied, staring hard into the rearview mirror.

"Let's go home," Deena said, feeling exhausted. "We'll be safe there."

Chuck turned the car up Park Drive and finally into the North Hills section of town where the Martinsons lived.

All three teens breathed in deeply when the car finally pulled into the circular driveway and Chuck cut the motor. For a moment they just sat in the car catching their breath.

Then they heard a squeal of brakes and the sound of a car roaring up the hill toward the house. Feeling a chill run down her back, Deena looked down the road and saw headlights approaching fast.

"Oh, no!" cried Chuck. "It's him!"

chapter

9

"*G*et inside!" ordered Chuck. "We'll be safe there." The three teens scrambled out of the car and onto the porch. But before they could get inside the car roared straight toward them up the driveway, sending the gravel flying, its headlights glowing like the eyes of some evil animal.

But instead of stopping, the stranger's car went all the way around the driveway, then sped away, heading back down Pine Road toward town.

"He's gone," said Jade, her voice trembling.

"Let's go in," said Chuck. "We're safe now."

Deena followed the others in. She wished her parents were home. Even more, she wished her hands would stop shaking.

Chuck was already at the phone dialing 911. "Hello," he said. "Send an ambulance to eight eighty-four Fear Street. A woman has been stabbed. My name? Just say I'm—the Phantom of Fear Street." He hung up.

"Chuck!" said Deena, dismayed. "Why'd you say that?"

"I can't give my real name," he said. "I'm in enough trouble already. They'll want to know what we were doing at the house. What would I say?"

"But what about the man?" Deena protested. "Shouldn't we report him?"

"We didn't see his face," Chuck pointed out. "We can't identify him—but he knows where we live. We'll just have to hope the police catch him."

Deena felt funny about not doing more, but she decided Chuck was probably right. The night's events had thoroughly exhausted her, and she yawned. Chuck had moved onto the couch beside Jade and was gently stroking her hair. Deena was surprised to see tears drying on Jade's face.

"This was the worst night of my whole life," Jade said. "I hope I wake up soon and find out it was all a nightmare!"

"It was real, all right," said Chuck, "but it's over now."

Deena saw Jade relax at Chuck's soothing words. But she couldn't help wondering if he was right.

Was it really over?

Later that night Deena awakened from a deep sleep, the sound of car tires squealing in her ears. Her heart began thudding, but then she relaxed. I must have been dreaming about what happened, she thought.

She wondered if Chuck and Jade were having nightmares, too. She and Chuck had driven Jade home just before midnight. When they'd returned Deena's parents still weren't home. Deena had collapsed into her bed and immediately fallen asleep.

But now—there it was again.

A car was crunching the gravel in the driveway.

A car door slammed, and then someone walked up the driveway toward the house.

Oh, no, no, Deena pleaded silently. Don't let it be the man in the mask—please. . . .

The doorbell rang. A moment later someone began pounding on the front door.

Deena lay in her bed, too scared to move. Then she heard her father's sleepy voice: "Just a minute!" Then his footsteps started down the stairs. "Just a minute!"

"Daddy, no! Don't answer it!" Deena jumped out of bed and ran down the hall, but it was too late. Her father had slid the chain back and was already opening the door.

Wildly, Deena searched around for a weapon. All she could find was a large green vase on a stand at the top of the stairs. Her hands trembling, she grabbed it, then began to creep down the stairs.

As the door swung all the way open Deena expected to see the man in the mask standing on the porch. But instead there were two men dressed in suits. One was tall and skinny, the other short and pudgy. They looked like a comedy act.

"Mr. Albert Martinson?" said the tall man.

"That's me," said Deena's father.

"I'm Detective Frazier from the Shadyside Police Department," the tall man said. "This is my partner, Detective Monroe. We're sorry to disturb you at such a late hour, but this is very important. Do three teenagers live here—a boy and two girls?"

"There are only two," said Mr. Martinson. "A boy and a girl. What's this all about?"

"May we speak to them, please?" said the tall policeman.

"Do you know what time it is?" said Mr. Martinson. "They're sleeping. Now, why don't you—"

"We just want to ask them a few questions," said Frazier. "Please, sir. We don't want to have to insist."

"All right, all right," Mr. Martinson mumbled.

While Deena watched, he stepped back to let the two men in. At first she had been relieved to see the detectives instead of the masked stranger, but her relief was now replaced by a new kind of fear. She didn't know exactly what was going on, but she had an idea it meant trouble.

She set the vase back on the stand and went downstairs.

"Daddy?" she said.

Mr. Martinson put his arm around her protectively. "These gentlemen are detectives," he said. "They want to ask you and Chuck some questions."

By now Mrs. Martinson had awakened and come downstairs. She was wearing a silver-colored bathrobe. With her thick golden hair frizzed around her face she looked like a movie star, Deena thought.

"Albert, what's going on?" she asked.

"These detectives want to talk to Deena and Chuck," he said.

"At two in the morning?" Mrs. Martinson protested.

"They say it's important," her husband answered.

"Come on in the kitchen," said Deena's mother. "I'll make coffee."

Deena's father went to the door leading to the basement and called Chuck's name. "There's someone here to see you!" he said.

After a few moments Chuck stumbled up the steps and into the kitchen, rubbing sleep out of his eyes. He had thrown on a pair of faded jeans and a green T-shirt. When he first saw the policemen his eyes filled with fear. But then, as Deena watched, the fear was replaced by a look of challenge—and arrogance.

Deena's mother had made the coffee. "Won't you sit down?" she asked the policemen.

"Thank you, ma'am," said Monroe. "You go on ahead." He and Frazier remained standing by the back door.

Deena's mother sat at the big kitchen table next to Deena. Both her parents looked worried, but the detectives had no expressions on their faces at all.

What is going on? Deena wondered. Obviously it had something to do with what had happened on Fear Street that night. Maybe the police wanted her and Chuck as witnesses. But how had they found them?

While Detective Frazier took notes his partner asked Chuck and Deena their names and ages and where they went to school. Then his expression became very serious. "Where were you this evening between nine-thirty and eleven P.M.?" he asked.

Deena opened her mouth to answer, but Chuck spoke before she could say anything. "We were right here," he said. "We barbecued some hamburgers, then just hung out and watched TV."

Deena shot Chuck a questioning look, but he

wouldn't meet her eyes. And then she realized why he was lying. If her father found out what they'd been doing, Chuck would be in big trouble. Somehow she had an idea he was already in a lot of trouble!

The detective turned to her. "Is that right, miss?" he asked. "You were here?"

Deena swallowed hard. "Yes," she whispered.

"What's that?" said Detective Monroe. "Speak up."

"Yes," Deena repeated.

"Was anyone with you?" Frazier asked.

"No," said Chuck.

"Yes," said Deena at the same moment.

"Well?" said the detective. "Which is it? Yes or no?"

"No," Deena mumbled. "It was just us."

For a very long time neither policeman said anything. Then they exchanged looks. Finally Detective Frazier cleared his throat. "Does either of you know a Mr. or Mrs. Farberson of eight eighty-four Fear Street?" he asked.

"No," said Chuck. Deena looked at him desperately. She was starting to feel sick to her stomach. The lies were getting worse. The detective was leading up to something—but what?

"Has either of you ever talked to either Mr. or Mrs. Farberson on the phone?" Detective Monroe asked.

"No," said Chuck.

"Or visited them at their house on Fear Street?"

"No!" Chuck exploded. "We've told you we don't know any Farbersons! How many times do we have to tell you?" Deena looked at Chuck. He looked angry, but something about his expression wasn't right. Suddenly she realized that he was scared—as scared as she was.

Mr. Martinson got to his feet. "Officers, you've heard them," he said, his voice very angry. "My kids aren't liars. Now get to the point!"

Once again the policemen glanced at each other. "We've got a witness who contradicts you," Monroe said. "Are you sure you don't want to change your story?"

"We've told the truth," said Chuck. He was staring straight ahead, and Deena could see a muscle in his cheek twitching. Her father was standing by the sink, his hands clenched in fists, while her mother sat unconsciously shredding a paper napkin with her fingers.

Who is the witness? Deena wondered. Could it be Jade? But if it is, she's in trouble, too. Maybe the neighbors had seen something. But we didn't see any neighbors. We didn't do anything wrong, she reminded herself. No matter what, we're innocent.

Detective Frazier sighed. "Our witness is Mr. Stanley Farberson," he said. "According to him, you two and another teenage girl broke into his house and burglarized it. Then, when his wife came home unexpectedly, you murdered her."

Deena gasped in shock. "Huh?"

"That's crazy!" said Chuck. "In the first place, we weren't anywhere near Fear Street. In the second place, we have no reason to steal anything or kill anyone."

"He claims he saw you," said Detective Frazier. "He gave us a license number—and it checks with yours."

"But what about the burglar—" Deena blurted out.

"Deena, be quiet!" Chuck's voice cut her off.

"Just a minute, Detective Frazier!" Deena's father shouted. Even though he was wearing his ratty old bathrobe, Deena thought he looked fierce and dangerous. "Are my children being charged with a crime?"

"Charged?" said Frazier. "Not yet. But we have—"

"Hold it!" said Mr. Martinson, cutting him off. He looked at Deena. "Deena," he said, "did you do the things you're accused of?"

"Of course not, Daddy," she said. "What really happened was—"

Her father cut her off with a shake of his head. He turned to Chuck. "Chuck," he said, "did you do these things?"

"No," said Chuck, his face sullen. "I don't know anything about it."

Deena flashed a worried look at Chuck. Her father moved closer to Detective Frazier. "I don't know what happened tonight," he said, "but I do know my kids. They wouldn't do any such thing, and they wouldn't lie to me. I understand you're just doing your job, but they're not going to say another word without a lawyer."

Detective Frazier nodded as if he wasn't surprised. "I'm going to have to take them in," he said.

"For what?" exploded Mr. Martinson. "Because some crazy man thinks he saw them somewhere? You have no evidence—"

"We have enough to hold them for further questioning," said Frazier. "We've checked your car. The front bumper and tires are clotted with the green sandy clay that's found only at the end of Fear Street, where the Farbersons live. It's still damp. Your car was there recently." The detective paused rather sadly. He looked directly at Deena, then at Chuck. "Don't make this any more difficult than it already is," he said. "Come downtown now, voluntarily. If you don't, I'll have to come back—with warrants for your arrest!"

chapter

10

So far, so good.

His plan had been accomplished even better than he had hoped. For once, luck was on his side. Things were definitely going his way.

Now all he had to do was wait for another week.

Wait and do nothing else—unless someone tried to get in his way. If that happened—well, one more murder wouldn't be so hard. In fact, it would probably be easier than the first one.

chapter

11

The Third Week in September

*D*eena woke up Sunday afternoon at two. She lay in bed a moment, confused; then everything that had happened the night before came flooding back like a nightmare.

The detectives had put her and Chuck in the back of their unmarked car and taken them to police headquarters. Mr. and Mrs. Martinson followed in the BMW. The detectives told Deena's mother that her Honda would be impounded for evidence.

Just before they drove off Chuck had whispered fiercely to Deena, "Don't say anything, Deena. We're innocent. Anything you say will make things worse."

At the station house everything looked just the way it did in the movies. There was a gruff-looking, gray-haired desk sergeant and battered gray metal desks covered with papers. Even though it was so late at night there was a uniformed officer filling out a report and talking on the phone.

Deena had only a couple of minutes to check out the place, because soon after they arrived she and Chuck were separated, and she was taken to a small room with no windows. She sat at a battered table with a scarred linoleum top while the detectives began questioning her again. They kept asking her who the other teenager was who had been with them.

Deena wanted to tell the truth, but remembered Chuck's warning, and she didn't want to get Jade in trouble. After a few minutes Sidney Roberts, her father's lawyer, showed up.

He talked some legal jargon with the detectives, and after a while they went out of the room. She was so tired by then that she didn't care much what happened. She wondered if she was going to be put in a jail cell. At least there will be a place to lie down, she thought.

The next thing she knew, her father was shaking her. She had fallen asleep bent over the table with her hands cradling her head. "Come on, honey," her mother said. "We can go home now."

Deena stood up shakily, yawning. "What happened?" she asked.

"We're letting you go—for now," said Detective Monroe from the doorway. "But we'll want to talk to you again. Don't leave town."

Deena almost laughed. Sure, she thought. As if I had anywhere to go. But how do you run away from a nightmare?

She followed her parents through the halls of the building, then out into the chilly night air. To the east, the sky was getting lighter. She had never stayed up so late before. They walked out into the parking lot before she remembered. "Chuck!" she said. "Where's Chuck?"

"They've arrested him," said her father, sounding grim.

"What?" said Deena, suddenly wide awake with shock.

"This isn't the first time he's been in trouble with the police," her father went on, his voice weary and sad. "Last year in Center City Chuck and some other boys were caught joyriding in a stolen car."

"But," Deena protested, "that doesn't have anything to do with what happened tonight!"

Her father suddenly looked very old, very weary. "The police checked his file in Center City," he said. "There was a record of his fingerprints. And—it seems that they match the fingerprints on the knife that was used to murder Mrs. Farberson."

chapter

12

Deena stared out into the early-morning darkness as they rode home in silence. No matter how hard she tried, she couldn't keep the horrifying scene in the house on Fear Street out of her mind. Again and again she saw the ransacked living room, the woman lying sprawled on the floor, the knife—the blood.

She wanted to tell her parents everything. Maybe if she described it out loud, she would stop seeing it over and over in her mind. But how could she explain? Where should she start?

Her father was the first to interrupt the silence. "I just don't understand this at all," he said in a voice she had seldom heard. "If you and Chuck don't know anything about this, how could Chuck's fingerprints be on the knife?"

"I—well—" Deena could feel all of the horror welling inside her. She suddenly felt like a balloon about to burst.

"Well what?" her father asked impatiently.

Deena couldn't hold it in any longer. "Of *course* his fingerprints are on the knife!" she screamed. "But he didn't kill her! She was already dead! You've got to believe me! *You've got to!*"

Then she started to cry and couldn't stop.

"Calm down, calm down," her mother said softly. "We'll talk about this when we get home."

Her father continued to drive, staring straight ahead through the windshield, his eyes hard and cold in the rearview mirror.

Despite the hour, Jade came over as soon as Deena called her. "Maybe the two of us can explain it to my parents," Deena said, opening the door for Jade. "I don't think I can do it by myself."

For once, Jade looked terrible. Her eyes were red. She was as pale as a ghost. The old sweater she had thrown on had a hole in it and a stain on one sleeve. "Is Chuck really in jail?" she whispered to Deena as they headed into the kitchen to face Deena's parents.

"Yes. He was eighteen on his last birthday. That means they can try him as an adult."

"But he's innocent!" Jade cried. "What about bail? Can't your father get him out?"

"There's no bail for *murder* suspects," Deena replied. *Murder.* She couldn't believe she was saying that word out loud.

"You've got to help me," Deena said, squeezing Jade's hand. "You've got to help me convince my parents."

They walked into the brightly lit kitchen. Mr. and

Mrs. Martinson greeted Jade without smiling. Mrs. Martinson poured her a cup of coffee.

"Okay. You're both here," Mr. Martinson said, grim-faced. "Begin at the beginning."

Fighting back tears and sipping coffee with trembling hands, Deena and Jade told her parents everything. They started with the phone calls. They ended with their visit to Fear Street and the terrifying car chase that followed.

For a long while after they had finished Deena's parents didn't say anything. They contemplated the floor, shaking their heads.

"Do you mean to say that this whole thing began with a prank phone call?" Mr. Martinson said at last.

"And it ended in a murder," Jade said sadly, her voice a whisper.

"But the two aren't connected!" said Deena, sighing miserably. It was hard to believe that those silly calls to Rob Morell and the others had started only two weeks earlier.

It seemed more like two years.

"We didn't mean any harm, Mrs. Martinson," Jade said. "It was just something to do—a fun way of putting on some of the boys at school."

"I just don't understand. Then how did Chuck get involved in it?" asked Deena's mother.

"He happened to overhear one of the conversations," said Jade. "And then he—uh—made some prank calls himself. But that isn't even how he happened to call the Farbersons' number."

"What do you mean?" asked Mr. Martinson.

"Well, you see, there was this bat," Deena said.

"A bat?" cried her mother, exasperated. "Deena, will you please try to make some sense?"

Deena sighed. She knew how lame the whole thing sounded. And if her parents wouldn't believe her, how could she expect the police to?

"It's obvious the girl is trying to protect her brother," Detective Monroe whispered to Detective Frazier, loud enough for Deena to hear. It was late Sunday afternoon. Deena and Jade had just told the whole story again, from the beginning. But from the expressions on the detectives' faces it was obvious that they only believed parts of it—the parts that seemed the worst for Chuck.

"Let's go over this again," said Detective Frazier. "When did Chuck make the threatening phone calls— before or after he made the bomb threat?"

"You make it sound so terrible!" said Deena, trying not to cry again, trying to maintain control. "But it was just a prank. And he didn't make all that many calls!"

"Even one bomb threat is a serious matter," observed Detective Frazier. "And you say he used the name 'The Phantom of Fear Street'?"

"On one or two calls," said Deena.

"Someone using that name called nine-one-one right after the break-in at the Farbersons'," Frazier said.

"That was Chuck," said Jade.

"Why did he use that name?" asked Frazier. "If he hadn't done anything wrong, why didn't he say who he was?"

"Because—we've *told* you!" Deena was so exasperated she felt like screaming. "He was already in enough trouble. He'd been expelled from his old school, he'd gotten in that stupid fight in the cafeteria—"

"A real model citizen, in other words," said Frazier sarcastically.

"Let's move on," said Detective Monroe, "to the night of the murder. Now, you say that Chuck just happened to pick the Farbersons' number out of the phone book at random?"

"That's right," said Jade and Deena in unison.

"And he did this because you girls were scared of a bat?" Disbelief showed on his face.

Deena just nodded. No wonder the policemen didn't believe her. It all sounded crazy, even to her. And yet it was true.

"Then you kids decided to go over to Fear Street—alone?"

"We thought of calling the police," Jade said. "But Chuck said you'd never believe us. And he was right! You don't!"

"Uh-huh," said Detective Monroe. "So you went over there and broke in the back door—"

"The back door had already been broken into," said Deena.

"Right," said Monroe. "And then you discovered the body of Mrs. Farberson."

"We didn't know who she was," said Deena.

"Chuck thought she might still be alive," Jade added.

"So he started to call for an ambulance," said Deena.

"And that's when your mythical masked man appeared," said Detective Frazier.

"He's not mythical!" said Deena. "He's real! He broke in and robbed the house. He stabbed Mrs. Farberson. He was still there when we arrived! Why aren't you out searching for him instead of putting Chuck in jail?"

"Farberson identified Chuck in a lineup this afternoon," said Monroe in a flat tone.

"Chuck's fingerprints were found on the murder weapon," said Frazier. "No one else's."

"But we explained that!" said Deena. "When the man in the mask—oh, what's the use?" She blinked back tears, then stole a peek at Jade. Jade appeared to be every bit as upset as Deena felt. She looked slightly green, as if she was about to become sick.

For a few moments neither policeman spoke. Then Monroe started in again. "Can either of you explain to me why a burglar—let alone a murderer—would hang around when he heard three people enter the house?"

"It doesn't make any sense," added Frazier. "Why would he let you see him? Why wouldn't he hide somewhere till you left? Or try to escape without being seen?"

"Why would he want to chase you?" said Monroe. "If he'd done the things you say, girls, he wouldn't be too interested in chasing after three teenagers in his car and then just driving away."

"We don't know why!" Deena shouted. "But everything we've told you is the truth!"

Detective Monroe sighed. "Listen to me, Deena— Jade. Loyalty is wonderful. I try to teach it to my own kids. But loyalty is no virtue when it causes you to lie to protect someone bad. Now, we understand that you want to help Chuck, but this crazy story can't do him any good at all."

"It's not crazy," Deena said. "It's true."

"Come on, girls," Detective Frazier said. "This has to be hard on you. You can help Chuck most by telling us the truth. So please, think carefully, and then tell us what really happened."

chapter

13

*S*unday night Deena couldn't get to sleep. The events of Saturday night and Sunday kept chasing through her mind. It was bad enough that the police didn't believe a word she and Jade had told them; now she had to go to school and face her friends, who would all know that she and Jade and Chuck were mixed up in a murder.

Monday morning she met Jade in the parking lot before school. Jade was wearing a navy jumper with a fuzzy pink wool jacket. She was dressed like her old self. For once, however, her mouth wasn't turned up in a mischievous smile—she looked grim.

"Have you seen this?" she said, handing Deena the morning paper.

Deena opened it. There was the story, right at the top of page one. The headline, in bold black letters, said:

LOCAL TEEN CHARGED IN MURDER

Below that, in smaller type, was a subheadline:

18-Year-Old Suspect Tied to Phone Threats

Her heart pounding, Deena began to read:

Charles A. Martinson, the son of local telephone executive Albert B. Martinson, was arrested at his home early Sunday morning and charged with the stabbing murder Saturday night of Edna Lemley Farberson, 45. Mrs. Farberson, who moved to Shadyside only six months ago, was found by her husband, Stanley, 46, in their ransacked house at 884 Fear Street.

According to police sources, Mrs. Farberson surprised the suspect as he was burglarizing the house. A struggle ensued, and Mrs. Farberson was killed with a ten-inch-long knife that her husband identified as from their kitchen. Mr. Farberson told police that he arrived home as the suspect was fleeing. "The moon was right above the house, so I got a good look at him and the license on his car," Farberson said.

Farberson didn't pursue the intruder but instead ran inside to check on the safety of his wife.

Farberson had come home early from Alberga III, a popular Italian restaurant that he owns and operates.

"Usually I don't get home till after midnight," Farberson told the *Press*. "But Edna wouldn't answer the phone, and I got worried. I had a feeling something was wrong."

The Martinson youth is being held without bail pending further investigation. Also arrested were two juvenile girls who were later released to their parents' custody. According to police sources, the three teens are implicated in a number of threatening phone calls that have been made in the Shadyside area in recent weeks, including the bomb threat at Shadyside Lanes last Saturday night.

These same sources report that Charles Martinson identified himself as the Phantom of Fear Street in these calls, while the girls made anonymous suggestive calls to local boys.

Deena finished reading the article, then reread it, hoping to find something different. Glumly she handed it back to Jade. "I'm not going to school today," she said, wishing she meant it.

"It's awful, isn't it?" said Jade. "But do you think anyone will know it's us?"

"Who else?" said Deena. "Chuck's my brother, and everyone knows you and I hang out together. I just can't figure out how Farberson saw Chuck. We didn't see him."

"Deena, we were running for our lives!" Jade answered. Then she looked at the paper again. "It says we were both arrested," Jade said. "But I wasn't even there!"

"It doesn't matter," said Deena. "The article makes everything look as bad as possible. People are only going to believe the worst."

"Like the police did," said Jade.

"Right," Deena agreed with a sigh.

* * *

As Deena and Jade had feared, the only topic of conversation at school that day was Chuck and the murder. Chuck had only attended Shadyside for two weeks, so just a few kids knew him. But by second period everyone in the school knew that he was Deena's brother, and that Deena and Jade were with him the night of the murder.

But strangely, no one seemed to blame the girls for anything. In fact, a lot of the kids seemed sympathetic. Deena was surprised in her first-period class when Kathy Narida passed her a note. "Don't worry," the note read. "Chuck's in my geography class, and I'm sure he's innocent."

Mostly, everyone was curious. They all wanted to know what had happened. Deena didn't know how Jade was handling it, but she tried to say as little as possible while still seeming friendly. It got stickier when Lisa Blume, assistant editor of the school newspaper, cornered Deena between second and third periods.

"I heard all about your brother," Lisa told Deena. 'Pretty rough."

"Yeah," said Deena. "Thanks."

"I'm sure he's completely innocent, though," Lisa went on.

"Of course he is," said Deena. She started to push past Lisa and head for her next class, but Lisa put her hand on Deena's arm.

"By the way," she said casually, "everyone says you and Jade were with Chuck when it happened. The *Spectator* would really love to do a feature on it."

"I'm sorry," said Deena, "but the detectives told us not to talk about it."

"Don't you want to let people know your brother is innocent?" said Lisa.

"Of course I do!" said Deena. "But—but every time I try to help him I end up making things worse! Please, Lisa, don't push me!"

"Sorry," said Lisa. "I understand. But maybe you can tell me a little bit about the other parts of it—that don't have to do with the murder."

"What do you mean?" said Deena.

"Well, what about the phone calls?" said Lisa.

Deena felt her heart sink. "It was just harmless fun," said Deena. "It didn't have anything to do with the murder—not really."

"Can you tell me the names of the people you called?"

"No!" said Deena. Then she smiled, hoping that she sounded casual. "Honestly, the police told me not to say anything. It was no big deal, really! Now, excuse me. I've got to get to class."

"Me, too," said Lisa. "But when it's all over, will you give me an exclusive?"

"Sure," Deena promised. If it's ever over, she thought.

In trigonometry class Deena was only half there while Mr. Spencer talked about sines, cosines, and tangents. All she could think about was what had happened Saturday night and the terrible trouble Chuck was in. Over and over her thoughts came back to the large man in the mask.

The burglar. The real killer.

If she could somehow find him, then maybe the police would let Chuck go. How could she find him? Where would she begin?

She was still thinking about the masked man after class when someone bumped into her, hard, in the hall. She raised her eyes, startled and annoyed, to see Bobby McCorey glaring down at her.

"Excuse me," she mumbled, even though he had bumped into her. She started to move on, but he stepped to the side, blocking her path. Now she could see that his two buddies, Eddie Mixon and Ralph Terry, were right behind him.

Even more annoyed, Deena glared back at Bobby. What was wrong with him? He hardly knew her. In fact, they probably hadn't said three words to each other in their whole lives.

And then she remembered.

Bobby was the boy Chuck had fought with the first day of school. Even worse, he was the first one Chuck had called claiming to be the Phantom of Fear Street.

"Will you let me get by?" Deena said, trying to sound polite but firm.

"Sure," said Bobby. "After you listen to me."

"All right," said Deena, trying to sound tough. "I'm listening."

"I want you to give your brother a message, Deena," Bobby said. "Tell the 'Phantom of Fear Street' that if he ever gets out of jail, his troubles aren't over. Got that?"

Deena didn't answer. "Just give him that message," Bobby repeated. "Of course, he probably won't ever get out. In fact," he added in a nasty tone, "according to the papers, he's guilty. And that means life in prison."

A film of tears suddenly formed over her eyes, and she didn't even notice that Bobby had turned away and gone off down the hall, laughing with his two buddies.

In a daze, Deena stumbled toward the lunchroom and got in line. Usually she was one of the first ones there, because she liked to get eating over with to go outside on nice days, or to go to the library when it was cold or raining. But that day she was nearly at the end of the line. She pointed at random to some things on the steam table, then took her loaded tray over to where Jade was sitting alone.

"I thought maybe you were staging a hunger strike," said Jade. "I'm almost finished eating already."

"If you're still hungry, you can have mine," said Deena. "I don't have much appetite today."

"I know what you mean," said Jade. "Nobody can talk about anything but the murder."

"And the phone calls," agreed Deena. She took a bite of some brown and green stuff on her plate and swallowed without really tasting it.

"That reminds me," said Jade. "I ran into Rob Morell this morning. He asked me if I knew anything about some sexy phone calls he got."

"Oh, no," said Deena. "You didn't tell him—"

"All I told him was that *I* didn't call him," Jade said.

"But the paper said the two of us—"

"As a matter of fact, I think he wants to discuss it

with you," said Jade. "Look. He's coming over here right now."

Deena saw Rob Morell, a friendly smile on his face, approaching with a tray in his hands. In a total panic she stood up, desperate for a way to escape.

"Sit down," said Jade. "You haven't eaten a thing." She pushed back her own chair. "Sorry I can't stay and talk to you guys, but I've got to return a library book."

"Jade, no!" said Deena. It was too late. With a flash of her mischievous smile Jade had turned and walked off. A moment later Rob Morell slid into the empty seat.

"Hi, Deena," he said.

"Hi," she mumbled. She sneaked a look at him. He didn't seem to be angry, or upset, or anything except friendly.

"I heard about your brother," he said. "What a drag."

"He's innocent," said Deena.

"Well, sure he is," said Rob. "I mean, I don't really know him, but he seems like a nice guy."

Deena didn't answer. As always when she was with boys, she couldn't think of a thing to say.

"You know," Rob went on, "I've been wanting to talk to you ever since we were in solid geometry together last year. Want to get together sometime?"

"I guess so," said Deena, not believing what she was hearing.

"You're probably pretty busy till the trouble with your brother gets taken care of," said Rob. "But I'll give you a call, if that's all right."

"It's fine," said Deena.

"Great," said Rob, standing up. "Somehow I have an idea I'll like talking to you on the phone!"

Later that night Deena tried to concentrate on her trig homework, but it was impossible. No matter how hard she tried to do a problem, her mind skipped to thoughts of Chuck or of Rob Morell.

In fact, Rob Morell was the first thing she'd been able to think about besides Chuck's trouble. What did he mean he wanted to talk to her on the phone?

Did he know she'd made those calls? Did he think she was after his bod?

Or maybe did he just like her? After all, he had said he'd wanted to talk to her since solid geometry class. And, she remembered, he had smiled at her sometimes during class last year.

Deena yawned and shut her trig book, then started to get ready for bed. When the phone rang she jumped nervously before grabbing up the receiver.

"Hello?" she said, hoping it was Rob.

It was Jade, her voice excited and urgent. "Deena, turn on your TV! Channel seven! Right now!" And she hung up.

Puzzled, Deena switched on the little set she kept on her desk. It was the local news, and a reporter was interviewing a big man with a broken nose. There was something familiar about the man. Deena was sure she didn't know him, but she had a feeling she had met him somewhere.

"What are your feelings about the suspect?" the reporter was saying.

"I hope he gets the maximum!" said the man in a deep, growling, strangely familiar voice. "I know I'm supposed to turn the other cheek, but I can't forgive someone for such a terrible crime.''

''Well, that about wraps it up here,'' said the reporter. ''Thank you, Mr. Farberson. Now back to the studio.''

Deena stared at the television.

Mr. Farberson?

Now she knew where she had seen him before.

She recognized his voice.

Mr. Farberson was the man in the mask!

chapter

14

*D*eena called Jade back right away.

"Was that who I think it was?" she said as soon as her friend answered.

"It's definitely him," said Jade. "I'd never forget *that* voice."

"Me neither," agreed Deena. "I think we ought to tell the police."

"Oh, sure," said Jade bitterly. "They didn't believe a word we said. And if they didn't believe us before, what makes you think they'll believe us now? They'll probably just think we're desperate, which we are."

"But it was him, Jade!" said Deena. "I'm going to call Detective Frazier first thing in the morning."

"Lots of luck," said Jade. "Especially since the police don't even believe there *was* a masked man."

"Well, we saw him," said Deena. "If it was Mr. Farberson, that means he broke into his own house."

"And murdered his own wife," Jade added in a soft voice.

"Why would he do such a thing?" said Deena.

"I don't know," said Jade. "There must have been a reason."

Deena sat thinking for a moment, wondering what reason anyone could possibly have for committing such a terrible crime. "Maybe he and Mrs. Farberson had a big fight," she said finally.

"Maybe," agreed Jade. "And maybe he killed her during the fight. But why would he break into the house? It doesn't make any sense."

"Wait a minute," Deena said. "What if that's the reason he did it?"

"Huh?" said Jade. "You lost me on that last turn."

"What if he broke into the house to make it look as if a burglar did it? What if it was all part of a plan to kill his wife?"

Jade was silent for a moment. "I see what you mean," she said. "But why would he want to kill her?"

"I don't know," said Deena. "But I'm sure the police can find out, and then they'll have to let Chuck go."

"I guess so," Jade said doubtfully.

"Sure they will. You'll see. And then we can forget about this whole thing and start living normal lives again." *If* the police listen to me, she thought. And somehow she didn't feel as sure of that as she sounded.

"Now let me get this straight," Detective Frazier said slowly. It was early the next morning, and Deena had intended to leave the detective a message, but he answered his own phone. From the skeptical tone in his voice she almost wished he hadn't. "You and your friend both contend that the masked man you claim to have seen at the Farbersons' place was actually Mr. Farberson?" Frazier went on.

"We're positive," said Deena. "When we saw him on TV last night we both knew—instantly—from his voice. It couldn't be anyone else."

"His voice," Frazier repeated dryly.

"And since it was him," Deena went on, ignoring the detective's lack of response, "that means he did it—broke into the house and killed his own wife."

"Does your voice analysis tell you *why* Mr. Farberson allegedly committed these crimes?" asked Frazier.

"I don't know. Maybe his wife had a big insurance policy," said Deena. "Or maybe they just had a fight. I'm sure you can find out."

"You are, are you?" said the detective. He was silent a moment, then he sighed. "That's an interesting story you've dreamed up," he said. "But that's all it is—a story. For your information, Mr. Farberson is a respected businessman in this town. I understand your desire to divert suspicion from your brother, but we're not buying any tall tales today."

Deena hung up the phone, feeling sick. Jade had been right—the police wouldn't listen to them. That meant it was up to her and Jade to prove that Mr. Farberson was the masked man. But how?

She yawned and finished getting ready for school before calling Jade. "What are we going to do?" she asked with a sigh when she had finished telling her friend what the detective had said.

"I'm not sure," said Jade. "Meet me at my locker before lunch. I think I'm getting an idea."

Just before lunch Deena found Jade bent over her locker stuffing two huge boxes into the tiny space.

"Hi," Jade said, looking up. "We definitely ought to campaign for bigger lockers."

"What in the world have you got in there?" said Deena.

"Props," said Jade.

"Props?"

Jade managed to get the locker door shut and clicked her lock on it, then looked at Deena with her familiar mischievous smile. Jade, Deena thought, was definitely up to something. But what?

Jade went right on, sounding excited and pleased. "Right after we talked this morning I reread the piece in the *Shadyside Press*," she said.

"I never want to see that again!" said Deena. "It's the worst newspaper article I've ever read."

"It's full of information about Mr. and Mrs. Farberson, though," said Jade. "For instance, it says that he owns and operates the Alberga Three."

"So?" said Deena.

"So," said Jade, "what better place to find out more about Mr. Farberson than the place where he works?"

"You mean go into the Alberga and talk to him?" said Deena. "Are you crazy?"

"Some people think so," said Jade. "But this idea is smart. Look, Deena, he's the owner and manager.

The article said he came home early Saturday night. That means he's probably not there during the day."

"I'm beginning to catch on," said Deena.

"Right," said Jade. "We'll drive over there right after school gets out. My dad's out of town, so I have the 'vette. We'll just poke around. See if we can find out anything."

"I don't know," said Deena. "It still sounds kind of dangerous. What if he comes in early? Don't forget he knows who we are."

"True," said Jade. "But he thinks I'm a redhead with long hair, and you're a blond with a layered cut."

"We are," said Deena, beginning to feel exasperated.

"But we won't be this afternoon," said Jade. She gestured toward her closed locker. "I stopped by my mother's beauty shop this morning before school and borrowed a couple of wigs. I told her we needed them for a Drama Club production." She smiled impishly. "Believe me, Deena, even our own parents won't know us—let alone Farberson!"

Deena met Jade in the Drama Club room after school. She had left a message for her parents that she had to go to the library.

Squinting into the brightly lit makeup mirror, the girls put on the wigs and extra makeup. When they had finished Deena thought they both looked great. Jade was now a blond with a bubble cut and green eyeshadow, while Deena had curly auburn hair in a frizz. Jade dotted a beauty mark on Deena's cheek with an eyebrow pencil.

"We both look at least eighteen now," said Jade. "Come on, this will be a snap."

The Alberga III was a few miles away, in the Old Village. Jade had never been in it but knew her parents ate there sometimes.

Despite the disguises, Deena felt a nervous knot begin to grow in her stomach as Jade pulled her red Corvette into a parking place right in front of the Alberga.

"I don't know, Jade," she said. "Maybe this isn't such a good idea. . . ."

"Listen," said Jade. "We have no choice. No one will believe us. We've got to get Chuck out of this mess. Now just follow my lead."

The Alberga III wasn't open for lunch, so the dining room was nearly empty. It was dark and cool looking, with big booths and banquettes covered in a dark, velvety cloth. On one wall was a large mural of Italy, and candles burned in glass holders at each table.

"Let's just order a pepperoni pizza to go," Deena cracked to break the tension.

"Get real," said Jade. "Now remember—keep your mouth shut and let me do the talking."

After a moment a tall, dark-haired woman came over to greet them. She was dressed in a white silk blouse and calf-length green skirt; she was as elegant as the restaurant.

"May I help you?" she said.

"We're here to apply for jobs," said Jade.

The woman looked at the girls, not hiding her surprise. "Did the agency send you?" she said.

"That's right," said Jade.

"But there's only one opening," the woman objected. "Mr. Farberson can't use more than one assistant."

"I'm the one applying," said Jade. "My friend just came along to keep me company."

"I thought you said—oh, never mind," said the tall woman. "You look a little young, but we're fairly desperate since Miss Morrison quit last week. You do take dictation and do bookkeeping?"

"Absolutely," said Jade.

"Then come with me," said the woman. "You can fill out the forms in the office."

Jade turned and winked at Deena, then both girls followed the tall woman through the restaurant kitchen into a small corridor. The woman knocked on a closed door, then called, "Mr. Farberson?"

"I thought he worked at night!" said Jade in a panicked-sounding voice.

"He has to get an early start," said the woman. "In fact, that's one reason we need an assistant at night." She knocked again.

Deena and Jade exchanged a quick glance. Deena got ready to turn and run in the opposite direction, but before she could do anything the door opened.

There stood the man with the broken nose. The man identified on television as Mr. Farberson. The man that both Deena and Jade knew was the masked man.

"Yeah?" he said in his low voice.

"One of these young women is here to apply for Linda's job," said the woman. "The agency sent her."

"Oh, yeah?" said Farberson. He looked at Jade, hard, then turned and looked at Deena. Deena felt as if her heart had stopped beating.

Farberson took his time looking both girls up and

down. Then he spoke again. "How old are you girls?" he said.

"I'm nineteen," said Jade. "I have a business certificate from the Commercial School."

"Oh, yeah?" said Farberson. Deena was beginning to find his limited vocabulary annoying. "Well, you might as well fill out an application," he said.

Deena began breathing again.

"Just have a seat," Farberson said, indicating two battered folding chairs. He thrust an application form at Jade. "Fill this out," he said. "I'll be back in a few minutes." He turned to the tall woman. "Come on, Katie," he said. "Let's check the wine inventory before Ernie gets here."

Mr. Farberson and the tall woman left the office, shutting the door. Deena and Jade glanced at each other.

"I don't believe it," Deena said.

"Believe it," said Jade. "Now, quick—we don't have much time!" Quickly she scurried behind Mr. Farberson's large, littered wooden desk.

Deena followed her. "What are we looking for?" she said.

"I don't know," said Jade. "Anything. Especially anything that tells us more about Mr. Farberson."

"What a mess!" Deena said, looking at the clutter of papers. Almost at random she picked one up. "Here's a work schedule," she said.

Jade turned to look at it. "According to this, Mr. Farberson only works every other Saturday night," she said. "That means he was off last Saturday!"

"That's interesting, but it doesn't really prove anything," said Deena. "Jade, this is hopeless. What do you think we—"

"Shh!" said Jade. "Just keep looking!"

Both girls continued picking up papers, glancing at them, and then putting them down as neatly as possible, so Farberson wouldn't be able to tell they had gone through the desk. Nothing either one of them found seemed to have anything to do with Mr. Farberson or his wife. Deena glanced at her watch. They'd been there for almost ten minutes. Jade frowned, then started to open the drawers one by one.

"Hurry," said Deena. "He might come back any minute."

"I know," said Jade. "But I just want to find— Wait a minute. I have an idea."

"I hope it's a fast one," said Deena.

"Whenever my mother wants to hide something— like the extra car keys—she tapes them to the underside of a drawer. . . ." She began pulling the drawers out again and feeling along the undersides with her fingers.

"Hurry!" whispered Deena, wondering how old you had to be to have a heart attack.

Jade had searched the undersides of all but one drawer.

Deena heard a sound in the hall, then the muffled voice of Mr. Farberson calling something to someone named Ernie.

"Jade—"

"Aha!" said Jade. She had her hand under the drawer. "Wait a minute. I think I've found something!" Her expression changed quickly from triumph to defeat. "Just a wad of chewing gum."

Shaking her head sadly, she started to close the desk drawer when a sealed envelope caught her eye. It was from the Shadyside Travel Agency. She picked it up to examine it when the office door started to open.

Jade shoved the envelope into a pocket and scurried across the stained carpet to her chair just as Mr. Farberson entered the room. Deena forced herself to look at his face. And felt cold all over.

"All right, girls," Farberson growled, his face frozen in a mask of anger. "Let's stop playing games. I knew the truth as soon as I saw you!"

chapter

15

"*D*id you hear me?" Mr. Farberson repeated. "I said I know the truth."

Jade recovered her voice first. "I don't know what you're talking about," she said.

"Don't hand me that," Farberson growled. Deena thought he had the meanest face she had ever seen. She tried not to think about what he would do next—now that he knew who she and Jade really were.

To her surprise, he just walked behind his desk and sat down. He still looked angry, but not dangerous. In fact, he let out a big sigh. "Come on, girls," he said. "I know you're not the agency. I doubt if you're really eighteen. What's your game?"

Deena had never felt so relieved in her life. She tried to keep her face from changing but sneaked a peek at Jade.

Jade could be a great actress, Deena thought. She

was staring right back at Mr. Farberson, her eyebrows raised haughtily. "What makes you think I'm not from the agency?" she said.

"I wasn't born yesterday," said Mr. Farberson. "Neither was Katie, the hostess. She thought something was a little funny about you gals, so we called the agency. They haven't sent anyone today."

"All right," said Jade, "I'll tell you the truth." She made it sound as if she was doing him a big favor. "The fact is I heard about this job from my cousin. She's a friend of your last assistant, Linda Morrison. My cousin told me Linda wasn't working here anymore, and I need a job. I didn't know you were hiring through an agency till I got here."

Farberson continued to look at her, an almost admiring look on his face now.

"I got to admit you have spunk," he said. "I'm halfway tempted to try you out."

"Thank you very much," said Jade, "but I wouldn't want the job now. I could never be happy working for someone who is so suspicious."

"Hey, listen," said Mr. Farberson, "I've got to take care of myself, you know? You'd be surprised how many people try to take advantage."

"I'm sure I would," said Jade, her voice like ice. "Come on, Sally," she said to Deena. "Let's go find someplace a little more congenial."

With that she stood up, grabbed the application she had started to fill out, and headed for the door. Deena, her legs a little weak, followed her out the door, down the corridor, through the restaurant, and into the car. Neither girl said a word until they were a block away from Alberga III, and then Deena let out a whoop.

"Jade, you were fantastic!" she shrieked.

"I can't believe it!" Jade had finally let herself start to laugh. "When he said he knew the truth, I thought he meant—"

"I know," said Deena. "Me, too. I was scared to death. But you were cool as a cucumber."

"Are you kidding?" said Jade. "I thought my heart had stopped beating! But I knew I had to keep talking."

"How did you know his former assistant's name?" Deena asked.

"The hostess told us," said Jade. "First she called her Miss Morrison, and then Linda."

"Wow," said Deena. "I was so scared I wasn't even listening. I think you deserve an Academy Award." She laughed again. " 'I could never work for someone who's so suspicious,' " she said, mimicking Jade. "That was great! And the way you calmly kept going through his desk drawers."

"Which reminds me," said Jade, slamming on the brakes and stopping in front of the 7-Eleven. She reached into her purse and pulled out the envelope she had taken. Jade carefully opened the envelope and pulled out a sheet of folded paper.

"What is it?" said Deena.

Jade scanned the paper. "It's a plane reservation," she said.

"A *plane* reservation?" said Deena.

"Get this," Jade went on. "It's to Buenos Aires, Argentina. One way."

"Wow," said Deena. "It looks as if Mr. Farberson is about to take a trip."

"And he's *not* planning to come back," Jade added. "The ticket's for Saturday morning."

"Saturday!" exclaimed Deena. "This is Tuesday already. Jade, we've *got* to take this to the police."

"No, wait." Jade stared at the paper in disbelief. "The ticket reservation is for *two* people. Not one."

"Huh?" Deena grabbed the paper away from her and read it. "What does that mean?"

"I don't know. I guess it means he was planning to take his wife."

"On a one-way trip to Argentina?"

"Maybe they were planning to take a ship back or something," Jade said. She put a hand on Deena's shoulder. "Sorry, kiddo. This paper I stole is useless. It doesn't prove anything. We struck out. If we show this to the police, they'll laugh us out of the station."

"We've got to let the police know that Farberson is leaving the country in three days," Deena insisted.

"How are we going to explain how we know that?" Jade asked. "He's a respectable businessman, remember? And we're two lying teenagers who just ransacked his office."

Deena stared at the plane reservation in her hands. "But if Farberson leaves town, we'll *never* be able to prove that Chuck is innocent," she wailed. "What are we going to do?"

Jade thought about it for a long while. "We have to find out more about Farberson," she said finally. "Maybe Linda Morrison can help us."

"Who?"

"His former assistant," said Jade. "Don't you remember anything? She's the woman whose job I was supposedly applying for today."

"Oh," said Deena. "Right. But how can she help us? We don't even know her."

"Can you get a car tomorrow?" said Jade instead of answering. Her smile was back, and Deena knew she was hatching another plan.

"I don't know," said Deena. "My parents are still mad about the phone calls, and my mother's car is still being held by the police."

"Listen, we've got the whole day tomorrow—teacher conference day, remember? My dad's back tomorrow, so I don't have wheels. Try to get the car. Offer to drive your dad to work. Tell your parents you have to do some research at the big library in Waynesbridge."

"What are you talking about?"

"This may not be a term paper," Jade said. "But as far as Chuck is concerned, it could be the most important research you ever did."

"I don't believe we're doing this," said Deena. It was eleven in the morning, and she was so nervous about driving her father's BMW she was having trouble concentrating on what she was doing. Usually she loved to drive either of her parents' cars. But everything that had happened lately, combined with the thought of what she and Jade were about to do, had given her a severe case of butterflies.

"Will you relax?" said Jade. "Just keep your eyes on the road. Miss Morrison said we should turn right on Lakewood."

"What did you say to her?" Deena asked. "How did you get her to agree to see us?"

"I told her we're conducting a survey," Jade said smugly. "I figure we can find out more if we go in person."

"Great," said Deena. "First we're applying for a job, now we're doing a survey. I'm sick of pretending to be someone I'm not, Jade."

"This is the only way we can help Chuck," said Jade. "Besides, there's no reason why we can't use our real names. And we *are* trying to get information from her."

"How did you even find her?" Deena asked.

"I let my fingers do the walking," answered her friend. "There were only two L. Morrisons in the whole phone book, and she was the first one I called."

Deena just shrugged. Jade was right that what they were doing was the only way to help Chuck. But somehow she had a feeling it was also a big game to Jade, a chance for her to show off and play tricks on other people.

"Turn here!" said Jade. "It should be up in the next block."

Deena pulled up to the curb in front of Miss Morrison's house. It was a small, one-story wooden frame house with a cheery vase of flowers in the front window.

"Now remember," said Jade. "Let me do most of the talking."

"Right," said Deena. She picked up her clipboard and followed Jade up the front walk. The door was opened by a short, attractive woman with frosted blond hair and a pleasant smile.

"Hello, Miss Morrison?" said Jade. "I'm Jade Smith from S and S Research Associates. I talked to you on the phone yesterday afternoon. This is my colleague, Deena Martinson."

No wonder Jade is so good at this, Deena thought. Who else would think to use a word like *colleague?*

"You girls are both so young," said Miss Morrison. "Come on inside."

"We're students at the college," Jade said. "We do surveys part-time."

The two girls followed Miss Morrison into a small living room decorated in soft shades of beige and rust.

Jade sat down in an armchair and pulled out a pencil, very businesslike. Deena tried to copy her actions and expression but felt like an idiot.

"Our firm is doing a survey of the restaurant business in Shadyside," Jade told Miss Morrison. "We're concentrating on employer-employee relations. Now, we understand you were recently employed by the Alberga Three restaurant?"

"That's right," said Miss Morrison. "But how on earth did you know that?"

"We've already interviewed your former employer, Mr. Stanley Farberson," Jade said. "Can you tell me what kind of a boss he was?"

Deena thought that something changed in Miss Morrison's face, as if a dark shadow had passed over her attractive features. "He was okay," she said sharply. "Not a bad boss."

Jade pretended to write something on her clipboard. "What exactly do you mean by that?"

Miss Morrison seemed visibly flustered. "Just that. He was okay. Treated everyone all right."

"I see." Jade made another notation. She looked so serious and businesslike, she almost had Deena believing it! "Now, did you know his wife?"

"What?" Miss Morrison's cheeks flushed.

"His wife. Did you know his wife?"

"I'm sorry. Yes. You'll have to excuse me. I'm a little edgy today. I'm having a bad day, and it isn't even noon."

"Well, we won't keep you long," Jade said. "So you did know his wife?"

"She came into the restaurant sometimes." Miss Morrison stared at the flower vase in the window.

"How did she and Mr. Farberson get along?" Jade asked.

Instead of answering, Miss Morrison gave Jade a suspicious look.

Oh, no. Jade's gone too far, Deena thought.

"What does that have to do with the restaurant or employee relationships?" Miss Morrison asked. She started to say something else, but the phone on the table beside her rang.

She picked it up quickly. "Hello? Oh, thank goodness it's you, darling. I've had such a dreadful morning. I—oh." She suddenly remembered Deena and Jade were in the room. Standing up, she handed the receiver to Jade. "I'm going to go talk on the other extension. Please hang this up when I get on. I'll only be a moment."

"Sure," Jade agreed. She held the receiver in front

of her, waiting for Miss Morrison to pick up the other phone.

"Are you there?" a man's voice on the other end asked.

Jade froze.

She was sure she recognized the voice.

She put the phone to her ear. When Miss Morrison got on, Jade clicked the receiver button, but she didn't hang up.

"What are you doing?" Deena demanded.

"Sssshhh." Jade held a finger up to her lips.

"Oh, darling, I'm such a wreck," Miss Morrison was saying with emotion. "You've got to come take it away."

"But I'm on my way to the restaurant," the voice said.

Jade knew she was right. It was Farberson on the other end! She pressed the receiver to her ear.

"I can't have it in my house any longer. You've got to come take it away. Please, Stanley. Please. Come take it away. Please!"

"Well, okay," Farberson growled. "I'll be there in five minutes."

Five minutes?

Jade silently replaced the receiver. "Deena—we've got to get out of here!"

"What? How can we—"

Miss Morrison returned, appearing flushed and uneasy. "Sorry about the interruption." She sat down in her chair. "Now where were we?"

Jade and Deena abruptly stood up. "Afraid we've got to be going," Jade said, looking nervously out the window.

"But what about your survey?"

"Uh—there's been a mix-up," Jade said. "We were supposed to be somewhere else now. I made a scheduling error." She looked at her clipboard as if to confirm the error. "We'll have to come back sometime."

"Why don't we just go through it very quickly?" Miss Morrison asked. "I'm sure we can do it in five minutes or so, and it'll save you a trip."

"No, really," Jade insisted, glancing out the window, her face reflecting her panic. "Come on, Deena. We've got to scoot. We're really sorry, Miss Morrison. Thank you for being so understanding."

Ignoring the confused look on Miss Morrison's face, Deena followed Jade out the door. "Hey—what's your hurry?" she called as Jade ran to the car and slid into the passenger seat.

"Farberson will be here any minute," Jade said in a loud whisper.

That was all Deena had to hear! She practically dived behind the wheel, started the car, and backed down the drive.

"Go around the block and come back," Jade instructed.

"What?"

"Park about halfway down the block. We've got to see what Farberson does, what's going on here."

"What *is* going on here?" Deena demanded. "What did you hear on the phone?"

"She called Farberson 'darling,' " Jade said, keeping an eye out for Farberson's car.

"She did? You mean—"

"I mean something is definitely going on between

the two of them. She begged him to come over and take something away. She said she couldn't bear to have it in her house anymore. He groused about it, but he's on his way over."

"What on earth could it be?" Deena asked. She circled the block and parked across the street and a few houses down from Miss Morrison's house.

Seconds later Farberson's old car pulled up Miss Morrison's short driveway. "Duck. Duck down!" Jade whispered. "He might see us."

As they peered over the dashboard Farberson walked straight up to the house without looking left or right. Miss Morrison greeted him at the door, and the two of them kissed, a long, lingering kiss. Then she pulled him inside and closed the door.

"Wow!" Deena said.

"Double wow," Jade said. "The two of them are definitely an item."

"Do you think Miss Morrison is the reason Farberson killed his wife?" Deena asked.

"I don't know." Jade stared at the closed door to Miss Morrison's house as if it had some answers for her. "I just thought of something. The plane reservations to Argentina."

"What about them, Jade?"

"Maybe the second ticket is for Miss Morrison."

"You mean he plans to leave the country with her. Yes! It's perfect!" Deena said with growing excitement. "He killed his wife, and he plans to run away with Miss Morrison. Now we really have something for the police."

"No, we don't," Jade said, shaking her head. "All we have are a lot of guesses. Maybe Farberson's having an affair with Miss Morrison. Big deal. That doesn't prove he killed his wife. We haven't proved anything, Deena.''

''Well, then we've got to get the proof. Why are we sitting in this car? Shouldn't we sneak up and look in the window?'' Deena started to open the car door.

''No. Don't move. He's only staying for a second. He told her he was on his way to the restaurant.''

Just as she said that the front door opened, and Farberson appeared. They could hear him call good-bye to Miss Morrison, and then he closed the door behind him.

''What's he carrying?'' Deena asked.

Farberson had a small package in his hands. It appeared to be a paper bag tied up with string.

He lifted the lid on the small garbage can next to Miss Morrison's porch and started to deposit the package in it. Then suddenly he changed his mind. He replaced the garbage-can lid and carried the package to his car.

''That's very strange,'' Deena said, ducking low behind the steering wheel.

''He started to throw it away, then he decided to take it with him. What on earth could it be?''

They watched Farberson back down the drive.

''Follow him, Deena,'' Jade said. ''Let's see where he goes with that package.''

Deena started the BMW and eased it slowly after Farberson's car, staying more than half a block behind him. ''I know what it is,'' she said suddenly, turning the corner.

''What?''

"I know what's in the package, Jade. I just know it for sure."

"Well, come on. Don't keep me in suspense."

"It's his mask," Deena said, her eyes straight ahead on Farberson's car. "It's the mask and the bloody shirt he wore the night he killed his wife!"

chapter

16

"*L*ook out for that bus!"

Deena swerved to the right just in time. The angry bus driver leaned on his horn. "Sorry," Deena apologized to Jade. "I was so busy watching Farberson's car, I didn't realize I was over the line."

"We're almost to his restaurant," Jade said.

"I know I'm right about the package," Deena said, stopping for a light. "He had to hide the mask and the bloody shirt somewhere, right?"

"Right," Jade agreed.

"Miss Morrison was the perfect person to keep it for him."

"Yeah. Maybe," Jade said. "I *did* hear her say over the phone that she couldn't bear to have it in the house any longer. She begged him to take it. Maybe you're right, Deena. Maybe the mask *is* in that package."

"If I *am* right, we'll have all the proof we need,"

Deena said, smiling for the first time in a long while. "It'll prove to the police that we were telling the truth, and it'll free Chuck."

"Whoa. Slow down."

"But I'm so excited about—"

"No, I mean *slow down*," Jade said. "There's Farberson's restaurant. He's parking right in front."

Deena slammed on the brakes. Luckily there was no one behind her. She saw a parking spot across the street. Letting a van go by, she made a wide U-turn and pulled into it. Then both girls got out of the car and ducked low behind a bus shelter.

They watched Farberson climb out of his car and lock it. He had the brown package under his arm. He walked to a row of garbage cans on the curb.

"Great!" Jade whispered. "If he drops it in one of those cans, we can easily pull it out after he goes inside."

But once again Farberson changed his mind. Transferring the package to his right hand, he turned away from the curb and headed into a narrow alley that ran beside the restaurant.

"Come on—we've got to follow him," Jade said, looking both ways and then bounding across the street.

"But—but he'll see us," Deena cried, following her.

"Just keep against the wall," Jade warned.

They inched along the wall, following Farberson to the back of the restaurant. Stopping at the corner of the building, they watched him enter a small cement courtyard walled in by buildings on all four sides.

A tall yellow garbage dumpster stood in the center of the courtyard. Farberson scanned the area, as if not wanting to be seen. Jade and Deena pressed themselves against the dirty brick wall and held their breath. Farberson tossed the package into the dumpster, then quickly disappeared into a door at the back of the restaurant.

"Let's go get it," Deena whispered. She was nearly trembling with excitement. Her heart was racing so fast she could barely breathe.

"Ssshhh. Wait another minute," Jade said, holding her friend back. "Make sure he's gone inside for good."

The minute seemed endless to both girls. When they were sure the courtyard was deserted they nodded to each other and made a run toward the dumpster.

They were halfway across the courtyard when a man's voice called to them angrily. "Hey—what are you doing?"

Deena froze. It felt as if her heart had suddenly stopped. She turned around.

"What are you girls doing back there?"

The door to the restaurant's kitchen was open. Two men wearing white aprons were at a long counter chopping vegetables. One of them—the one who had called to them—stepped to the doorway.

"Uh—we thought the entrance was back here," Jade said, thinking quickly as usual.

The man chewed on a toothpick and eyed them both suspiciously. "We're closed," he said. "We're not open for lunch." He spit out the toothpick.

"Oh. Okay. See you later," Jade said. She followed Deena, who was already hurrying away.

They ran back along the narrow alleyway. Neither

of them said a word until they were safely back in the car and heading toward Deena's house.

"Close call," Jade muttered finally, still looking shaken. "That cook didn't look like a nice guy."

"What are we going to do?" Deena wailed. "We've *got* to get that package. We were so close! If only—"

"We'll go back," Jade said.

"But the kitchen door is open. That guy will never let us get to the dumpster."

"No. Not right now," Jade said, thinking hard. "We'll go back tonight. The cooks will be so busy they won't have time to notice two girls pawing through their garbage."

They drove on for a while in silence. "What do you think?" Jade asked finally. "Is that a good plan?"

Deena's features hardened. "We have no choice," she said quietly.

"Park as close as you can to the alley," Jade instructed, "just in case we have to make a run for it."

Deena felt a wave of fear run down her body. "Do you think we'll have to run?"

Jade shrugged. "Just being realistic. Don't look so scared. No one's going to do anything dreadful to us for going through a garbage dumpster."

"What if Farberson sees us?" She swerved to avoid a girl on a bicycle crossing the street against the light. "Wish these headlights were brighter. It's so dark tonight."

"There's no moon," Jade said, looking up at the sky through the car window. "It's nearly nine o'clock, Deena. I'm sure Farberson is really busy."

"I hope you're right," Deena said, unable to shake off her feeling of dread.

The restaurant came into view. "It's crowded tonight," Deena said, slowing down, searching for a parking place. "The places on that side of the street are all taken."

"Oh, well," Jade said, disappointed. "Park in that empty lot across the street. Maybe we'll get lucky and won't have to run for our lives."

"Very funny," Deena said, pulling into the lot and parking the car as near to the street as possible. "How come you're in such a breezy mood?"

"I'm not," Jade said seriously. "I'm just excited because I think you're right about that package. And if you are right and we do get the mask tonight, we'll be able to get Chuck out of jail—and the real murderer in!"

Deena held up her hands with both sets of fingers crossed. "Let's go."

A few seconds later they were making their way through the narrow alley. It seemed much narrower and longer in the dark, and much creepier. "Why didn't we bring flashlights?" Deena asked, walking against the wall right behind Jade.

"Flashlights would be noticed," Jade whispered. "Don't worry. There'll be enough light from the surrounding buildings once we get to the courtyard."

They came to the back of the building. The courtyard was illuminated by a single light bulb above the kitchen door, which both girls were thankful to see was closed. "That's a break," Deena whispered.

"Just pray that no one opens it while we're back

here," Jade said, and then she gasped and nearly fell backward into Deena.

"Jade—what's wrong?" Deena cried, startled.

"Something—something scampered over my feet. It—"

Deena looked down. A large gray rat scurried past them and disappeared in the dark alley.

"Oh, that was the *worst* feeling," Jade said, breathing hard.

"There must be more of them," Deena said, her voice trembling. "They probably come back here for the garbage."

"Oh!"

Another rat leapt off the top of the dumpster. It made a screeching noise as it hit the pavement, then scurried off in the direction of its companion.

"Come on, Deena. Let's see if the rats have left us anything."

As they approached the tall dumpster Deena gazed up at the buildings surrounding the courtyard. There were lights on in several windows. She hoped no one would accidentally see them down there.

"Come on," Jade urged. "It's too tall to see the bottom. We've got to climb in."

"What? Climb in?" Deena took a deep breath. The stench of rotting food filled her nostrils. "Ugh."

"You'll get used to it," Jade said, holding her nose. "I think. Come on. Give me a boost. I'll get in and then pull you up."

"It's disgusting," Deena complained, starting to feel sick. "I—I really can't stand the smell."

"Deena—forget about the smell. Snap out of it. Let's grab the package and get out of here."

"Give me a boost," Jade said.

Deena struggled to push her up to the top of the dumpster. Jade grabbed hold of the rim, pulled herself in, and then dropped to the bottom. "If you think it smells bad out there, wait till you get in here," Jade called.

"Do you see the package?" Deena asked hopefully.

"All I can see is rotting cabbage," Jade said. "They must've made a lot of coleslaw today!" She leaned over the side and offered her arms to Deena. "Come on. I'll help you in. We're both going to have to search."

"Are there—rats in there with you?" Deena asked, taking Jade's hands.

"Only a few," Jade answered dryly. She tugged, and a few seconds later Deena was beside her, also knee-deep in garbage. "Come on. Start searching."

They began pawing through the wet, rotting garbage. "This is so disgusting," Deena complained. "I'm going to have to take six baths when I get home."

"We'll have to bury our clothes," Jade said. "Now where is that package? It must be down near the bottom. Oh. These fish parts smell the worst!"

Suddenly they heard a noise. They stopped their search and ducked down low.

The kitchen door had opened.

Deena held her breath.

Someone was approaching the dumpster.

No, no—please go away, she begged silently.

Suddenly two big black plastic garbage bags came flying on top of the two girls. Jade toppled over into the garbage. Deena managed to remain upright. Neither of them made a sound.

The footsteps retreated. The kitchen door closed.

"Jade—where are you?" Deena whispered, shoving one of the garbage bags aside.

"Where do you think?" Jade's voice was muffled. "Oh, Lord. I'm covered in garbage. Why don't these people use garbage bags for *all* their garbage?" She started to pull herself to her feet, then stopped.

"What's the matter?" Deena asked. Some of the garbage at the other end of the dumpster was moving. She realized there must be a hungry rat down at that end.

"I felt something," Jade said, reaching down to the bottom. Then she smiled and held up the brown package. "Got it."

"Quick—open it up!" Deena cried excitedly. "Is it the mask?"

"No—not here," Jade said. "Let's get back to the car."

Deena quickly agreed. She jumped down from the dumpster, then helped Jade down. They looked at the restaurant kitchen, but the door remained closed.

With the odor of the garbage still in their nostrils they ran at full speed down the dark alleyway. As they reached the sidewalk they nearly collided with an old couple leaving the restaurant. "Watch where you're going!" the man cried. But they didn't stop running until they reached the parking lot.

Then they both leaned against the car and waited to catch their breath. "Open it. Come on," Deena demanded. "We did it, Jade. We got our proof. I *knew* we could get Chuck out of trouble!"

The package was tied very tightly. Jade struggled to

remove the string. "It feels too heavy to be a mask," she said.

"That's because his shirt must be in there, too," Deena said, watching Jade's efforts impatiently.

Finally Jade pulled off the string and tore open the paper.

Both girls screamed when they saw what was in the bag!

chapter

17

*T*he dead cat seemed to stare up at them. Its eyes had already sunk deep into its head.

It smelled worse than the dumpster.

Jade dropped the cat, still wrapped in brown paper, on the ground.

"I don't believe it," Deena wailed. "A dead cat. Farberson was throwing away a dead cat."

"Miss Morrison said she was having a bad morning," Jade recalled. "I guess her cat died. I guess she couldn't bear to deal with it. So she asked Farberson to do it."

"I don't believe it," Deena said again, shaking her head. It was taking a lot of effort not to burst into tears. "I'm so disappointed, Jade."

"Me, too." Jade leaned against the trunk of the car and closed her eyes. "I really thought you were right, Deena. I thought we had the mask. I thought—oh, what's the point?'' she asked bitterly. She glanced down at the dead cat at her feet and made a face.

"Now what?" Deena asked glumly. "What do we have for all our clever detective work?"

"Well, we know that Farberson plans to leave the country on Saturday. We know that he and Miss Morrison—"

"Nothing," Deena interrupted bitterly. "We've got nothing. No proof of any kind. No proof that he was the man in the mask. No proof that he killed his wife. Nothing."

"Well, maybe he didn't do it," Jade said thoughtfully.

"Huh?" Deena looked at Jade in shock.

"Maybe we jumped to the wrong conclusion because Farberson's voice is similar to the man in the mask's. But face it, Deena, we don't have any evidence at all. Just as you said."

"No. It was him that night. It was Farberson," Deena insisted. "I have no doubt about that."

Jade looked at her. "No doubt at *all?*"

Deena didn't reply. She sighed wearily. "Come on. Let's go home."

They climbed into the car. Deena searched in the dark for her keys. "Why don't they put some lights in this parking lot? It's as dark as that alley."

Jade shuddered. "Don't remind me of the alley."

Deena finally found the key and struggled to get it into its slot.

"Come on—let's get out of here," Jade said edgily.

"I'm trying," Deena whined.

She started the engine and put the car into reverse. She turned to look out the rear window as she started to back up—and a powerful hand reached out from the backseat and grabbed her shoulder.

"No!" she screamed, and she slammed on the brake.

Jade turned, her eyes wide with horror, and saw the man in the mask just as he grabbed her shoulder with his other hand.

"Ouch—you're hurting me!"

He squeezed their shoulders hard and pushed his masked face up close to them.

"Don't ever let me see you again," he said in a low, menacing growl. "I only give one warning."

His breath was hot and smelled of garlic.

He shoved them both hard from behind, then lurched from the car, leaving the back door open, and disappeared into the darkness.

chapter

18

*T*he next day Deena was barely able to sit through her classes. All morning long she kept hearing the masked man's voice repeating his warning in her ear. Her shoulder was still sore from where he had grabbed her.

Why didn't he kill us? she wondered.

Why should he? She answered her own question. He'll be long gone on Saturday, and Chuck will be here to pay for his crime.

Just before lunch she went to her locker. Struggling to open it, she dropped her armload of books. When she leaned down to pick them up her purse fell. Its contents poured out onto the floor.

"Need some help?" asked a familiar voice.

Deena stared up at Rob Morell, who was smiling in a friendly way. She was too tired and flustered to do more than stammer thanks. But Rob didn't seem to mind. He bent down and helped her stow her gear away, then asked her to have a Coke with him after school.

Deena felt like bursting into tears. "Thanks, Rob. But I have some things I have to do," she said.

Rob looked disappointed, then shrugged. "Well, maybe another time," he said, and he walked off down the hall.

Deena watched him go, feeling terrible, but how could she tell him what she had to do? How could she tell him that she had to go visit her brother in jail? Her poor brother, who was going to stand trial for a murder he didn't commit.

As she walked out of the building Deena felt guilty. She should have gone to see Chuck long ago, but she just couldn't bring herself to do it. She didn't want to see him there in that awful jail. She didn't know what she'd say to him.

But he had been asking about her. She really had no choice. She had to steel her nerves and face him. She had to tell him how the police wouldn't believe a word she said, and how miserably she had failed at being a detective.

The heavy metal door shut behind her with a clang that made Deena jump. Her heart pounding furiously, she followed the guard down a long, dark hall. The tile on the floor was discolored and scarred from the thousands of feet that had walked this same hall on the way to being locked up.

The hall passed through two more metal doors, then opened into a large, nearly empty, fluorescent-lit room.

"Please sit here," said the guard. "They'll bring your brother out in a minute." She gave Deena a big, friendly smile. Deena just stared at her. How could anyone be cheerful in a place like this?

The guard left Deena alone in the room. It was narrow and windowless, divided down the center with a long Formica-covered counter. From the counter to the ceiling wire screening extended to keep the visitors and the prisoners from touching each other.

At the farthest end of the room a young woman sat hunched over the counter, sobbing into a handkerchief. Deena couldn't see whom she was talking with but could hear the low, monotonous drone of a man's voice from the other side of the screen.

Her knees quaking, Deena took a seat on a beat-up wooden chair on the visitor's side of the counter. She'd never been in such a dismal place, and wasn't sure she wanted to be there now.

What would Chuck be like? she wondered. Would he look different? Would he act different—tougher, maybe? She felt so nervous, she wished she could just run away.

After endless minutes an armed guard led Chuck into the other section of the room, on the other side of the screen. He was wearing a light blue cotton shirt and dungarees, and Deena thought he looked pale and thin.

He didn't see her at first, but when he did he burst away from the guard and came running toward her. "Deena—"

She stood up to greet him.

"Stop right there!" the guard screamed. "You know the rules."

Chuck immediately stopped a few inches from the screen and slumped into the folding chair provided for prisoners. "No more fast moves, you hear?" the guard warned, crossing his arms over his chest and staring at them both.

"Chuck, hi," Deena said uncomfortably. She forced herself to look into his eyes. They were red-rimmed and watery.

"You've got to get me out of here," he said in a loud whisper.

"Huh?" She wasn't sure she'd heard correctly.

"I can't take it, Deena. I really can't. I'm going out of my mind." He closed his eyes and pressed his forehead against the screen.

"Back up!" the guard called, uncrossing his arms and taking a step toward Chuck.

"Sorry," Chuck called back to him loudly, and he sat up straight.

"Next warning and you go back to your cell," the guard said.

"It's terrible in here," Chuck said, keeping his voice low. "It's just a hundred humiliations a day. Most of the men in here are criminals. Real criminals. Robbers and drug dealers. And there's one guy who brags about how he killed a whole family of campers in the state park."

Deena stared at him, trying to keep the tears out of her eyes. "That's so awful," she managed to say.

"I've got to get out. I've *got* to! I can't believe this has happened to me. It just isn't fair!"

"Dad says the lawyer will get you out soon. He just has to get the charge changed to manslaughter," Deena said, but it sounded pretty lame even to her.

"It won't be soon enough," Chuck cried. "I've got to get out now!"

"Jade and I are trying to help," Deena told him.

For the first time Chuck's face brightened. "How is Jade?"

"She's worried about you."

"That makes two of us," he said glumly.

"Jade and I have found out some things," Deena whispered.

"Two more minutes," the guard interrupted, looking at the large round clock on the far wall.

Deena quickly told Chuck about Farberson, about the plane reservations, and about their trip to Miss Morrison's house.

"Whoa!" Chuck said. "You two really took a chance. I can't believe you did that for me."

"Well, you're my brother," said Deena. "Besides, Jade and I are involved, too."

"Yeah. But you're not behind bars," he said, turning bitter again. "Man, if only I were out of here. I'd go right to Fear Street, right to Farberson's house, and I'd search the place till I found the evidence I need to prove that he's guilty."

"Okay," Deena said.

"What? What do you mean okay?" He looked confused.

"Jade and I will go to his house."

"No—wait! I didn't mean for *you* to do it. I said *I* would do it if I were out."

"Well, we're out, and you're not, so we'll—"

"No way!" Chuck screamed. "No way! It's too dangerous! The man is a killer! No way! I won't let

124

you go there!" He jumped to his feet and pressed his hands against the screen.

"Hey—" the guard yelled.

"We're going, and you can't stop us!" Deena declared. "We only have till tomorrow night to prove he's guilty."

"No way! I won't let you do it!" Chuck screamed. "No way!"

"I warned you," the guard said, moving quickly. He grabbed Chuck with both hands and pulled him away from the screen.

"Let me go," Chuck snapped angrily at the guard and struggled out of his grasp. "I don't want you to go to Fear Street," he shouted to Deena.

The guard grabbed him from behind and started to put a choke hold on him. "Do I have to get rough, kid?"

"Get off me!" Chuck raged.

Deena couldn't bear it any longer. She stood up and turned away. The other guard appeared suddenly and led her out of the room. As the door closed she could still hear Chuck scuffling with the guard.

"Deena! Deena—did you hear me?" he was screaming after her.

chapter
19

*B*y the time she got home from the jail Deena felt awful. Her head ached, and she felt sick to her stomach. Maybe I'm getting the flu, she thought. Maybe I'll just go to bed and hide under the covers, and all this will go away.

But she knew it wouldn't.

The only way to make it go away was to go to Fear Street and prove that Farberson was the murderer.

At dinner she didn't feel like eating, and as usual her mother noticed. "What's the matter, honey?" she said. "Don't you feel well?"

"I'm all right," said Deena. To prove it she took a big bite of mashed potatoes. Usually they were her favorite, but that night they tasted like sawdust.

"I know what it is," said her mother. "You're worried about Chuck, aren't you?"

Deena nodded. She didn't trust herself to say anything more.

"We're all worried, Deena," said her father. "But remember that Chuck brought a lot of this on himself. If you kids hadn't made those fool phone calls—"

"He didn't murder anyone!" Deena shouted, surprising herself with her outburst. "He's not a criminal! But the police have him locked up like one, and now you're saying he deserves it!"

"Now, just a minute, young lady," said her father. "I did *not* say any such thing! I only meant—"

Deena didn't wait for him to finish. She pushed herself away from the table, ran upstairs to her room, and threw herself on the bed, sobbing. A few moments later her mother tapped on the door. "May I come in?" she asked.

"Help yourself," Deena mumbled.

Her mother sat on the edge of the bed and began to rub her back. "You mustn't be angry with your father," she said. "Don't you know how hard this is on him? After all, Chuck is his only son."

"I'm sorry, Mom. I just don't want to talk about it. I'm tired, and I just want to be left alone."

Her mother patted her and stood up with a worried look. "All right, honey," she said. "If you want to talk later, I'll be downstairs."

After a while Deena stopped crying and splashed water on her face. Then she sat down and tried to work on her trig homework, but she couldn't concentrate.

It was no use. No matter what she tried to think about, her thoughts kept coming back to one thing: She had to go to Fear Street.

The phone rang, and she jumped, her heart suddenly beating fast. What if it was *him?*

127

But it was Jade.

"How was Chuck?" she asked right away.

"Angry and bitter," said Deena. "But who can blame him? He said to tell you hi."

"How did he look?"

"Like a prisoner," said Deena irritably. "What do you expect?"

"You don't need to bite my head off," said Jade.

"Sorry," said Deena. "I guess all this is getting to me."

"Me, too," said Jade. "What are we going to do next?"

"I guess we're going to have to pay a return visit to Fear Street," Deena said.

Jade didn't say a word in reply.

Deena was so tired she managed to sleep well that night. And she woke up feeling refreshed and energetic—until she remembered what day it was and what she and Jade were going to do that night.

But maybe it wouldn't be so bad, she told herself. For one thing, Farberson would probably be working. They'd have all the time they needed to find something linking him to the murder.

At lunch Jade was actually cheery. "Ready for another adventure?" she said, setting down her tray.

It was hard to think of it as an adventure. But Jade's good mood relaxed Deena, and she felt even more cheerful when Rob Morell waved at her from across the cafeteria, then gave her a wink.

By the end of the day she felt nervous but confident. The only thing bothering her, in fact, was that it was beginning to cloud up outside. But what was a little rain?

By the time Deena got home from school it was pouring. The house was as dark as night; Deena's mother worked late on Fridays, and her father wasn't home yet.

Deena put down her books and was heating up some soup in the kitchen when the phone rang.

"Hello, Deena?" It was her father.

"Hi, Daddy," she said, trying to sound cheerful.

"Some weather, eh?" he said. "Listen, we've had some trouble down here at the phone company. Lightning struck a transformer, and the phones are out on the south side of town. Everyone's staying late till we get it straightened out. Tell your mother not to wait up for me."

"Okay, Daddy," she said. "Try to stay dry."

She quickly ate a bowl of soup, then changed into sweatpants, a warm jacket, and her rain poncho. Just before leaving she wrote her mother a note saying that she had gone over to Jade's house to study, then she walked down to the Division Street Mall, where she and Jade had arranged to meet. What a night to be without wheels, she thought.

By the time she got there she was drenched. Jade was waiting in front of the pizza restaurant wearing a bright yellow raincoat and somehow managing to look fashionable and dry at the same time.

"I feel like a drowned duck," Deena complained.

"You look like one, too," Jade agreed. "Ready?"

"I guess so," said Deena. "But let's call first and make sure Farberson's not home."

Jade dropped a coin into a pay phone, then hung up,

a frown on her face. "That's funny," she said. "I didn't get anything—not a ring, not a busy signal, just dead air."

"I forgot," Deena told her. "My dad called—the phones are out on the south side of town."

"Oh, no!" said Jade. "What'll we do?"

"We'll just have to go on over there," said Deena. "What choice do we have? If we see a light on, we'll think of another plan."

Jade nodded. "I'm sure he'll be at the restaurant," she said. "He wouldn't want to do anything unusual—not the night before he's leaving. Right?"

"Right," said Deena, hoping it was true.

The girls left the mall, then caught the Waynesbridge bus, which crossed Division Street, then went south on the Mill Road. The bus was warm and comfortable, and Deena tried not to think of where it was taking them.

Too soon, Jade nudged her. "It's the next stop," she said.

Reluctantly, Deena pulled the stop signal, and the bus pulled into a small roadside clearing. It looked deserted there, with thickly overgrown bushes and trees growing right up to the edge of the road. Water dripped everywhere, and though it was still early, the storm clouds were so thick it was as dark as midnight. Overhead the sky flashed with lightning, and the booming sound of thunder shook the ground. A stream splashed angrily along a ditch beside the Mill Road.

"Nice neighborhood," Jade cracked.

"Very funny," said Deena. She squinted through the gloom, then saw a street sign a few feet down the road. "This way," she said, and the girls slogged along the muddy shoulder to the crossroad.

One arm of the sign said, in rustic letters, "The Mill Road." At an angle, the other arm read: "Fear Street."

The girls exchanged looks. Deena hoped she didn't look as scared as Jade did.

"Hey, it's just a street, right?" said Jade, trying to smile.

"Right," said Deena.

chapter

20

Feeling wet and miserable, the girls began to trudge east on Fear Street toward the Farberson house. As she walked Deena tried to pretend she was on any other street in town. In all the rain, however, she had to admit Fear Street didn't look gloomier than any other street.

After they'd walked a little more than a block the rain intensified, and with it the howling wind. Overhead, lightning continued to flash.

"What was *that?*" Jade suddenly shrieked, grabbing Deena's arm.

Deena turned and saw *something*—something dark and sleek—disappear into a yard across the street. "Probably just a dog," she said. "Anyway, it's gone."

They continued walking, their feet squishing in the mud and water that cascaded along the broken pavement. "Shouldn't we be there by now?" Jade asked.

"There's the house," Deena said, pointing.

The Farberson house was completely dark. The two girls made their way up to the porch and looked into the living-room window. Too dark to see anything.

"He must be at the restaurant," Jade said. "Thank goodness."

Deena went to the front door. There was bright yellow tape across the door that said CRIME SCENE. She tried the handle, but the door was locked.

"We'll have to break the window and go in," Jade said.

"No. Not in front. Someone might see us. Come on. Let's go around to the back."

They hurried around to the back, slipping on the wet mud at the side of the house. The rain had slowed a little, but lightning continued to flare as they stepped up to the back door.

The glass in the kitchen door had not been replaced; the empty pane had been covered with a piece of cardboard, so soggy it nearly disintegrated when Deena pulled it off.

She put her ear to the empty pane.

There was no sound inside.

"Hello!" she called, ready to run if there was an answer.

The only reply was the whistling wind and the tapping of dripping water.

Carefully she reached her arm through the space and found the doorknob, then flipped off the lock.

"Okay," she said, slowing pushing the door in. "Let's go."

The girls exchanged frightened looks, then stepped into the dark and empty house.

The first thing Deena noticed was that Mr. Farberson hadn't bothered to clean up since the last Saturday night. The kitchen table was standing right side up, but the counter and floor were still covered with spilled spices and flour. Her flashlight beam showed mouse tracks in the powdery debris.

"Yuck!" she said. "This is disgusting!"

"If you think the kitchen's disgusting, you ought to see the living room," called Jade. Deena followed her friend's voice to the scene of the Saturday night horrors. Dark stains still showed on the carpet, and a bright yellow chalk line, left by the police, showed where Mrs. Farberson's body had lain. The floor was still littered with broken lamps and ashtrays, and Mr. Farberson hadn't even bothered to pick up the cushions scattered around the room.

"What a mess," said Deena. "I don't even know where to start."

"Do you see anything that looks like a desk?" Jade asked. "Maybe we'll find some papers—insurance, a diary—something."

The girls swung their flashlights across the room, but there was no sign of a desk or even a writing table.

"Look at this," said Jade, pointing with the beam of her flashlight. To one side of the couch lay a basketful of old magazines. "Hold the flashlight while I look through these," she said.

Jade knelt and rapidly flipped through half a dozen periodicals. There were several issues of a weight-loss magazine and something called *Your Modern Home*, with mailing labels addressed to Mrs. Edna Farberson.

"Well, that was helpful," Jade said, brushing dust off her hands.

Deena went to the telephone stand, which contained only the phone and phone book. She pulled on the drawer, but it was stuck. In frustration she pounded on it and pulled again with all her strength. The drawer suddenly came loose, sending the telephone clattering to the floor. Jade let out a little shriek. "Will you be *careful?*" she said.

"I think I've found something!" said Deena, suddenly excited as a small white notepad fell out of the drawer. She picked it up and examined it under the flashlight. "False alarm," she said. "It's completely blank."

"Wonderful," said Jade. "Come on, let's try upstairs."

As they began to walk up the old, creaking stairs Deena heard a noise that caused the chill to return to her spine. "Do you hear that?" she whispered.

Now Jade, too, stopped. "That creaking sound?"

"It sounds like someone in a rocking chair," Deena said. "Do you suppose—"

"But who could it be?" said Jade. "Mr. Farberson's at work, and Mrs. Farberson's dead."

What am I doing here? Deena thought.

"It's probably nothing," she said, trying to convince herself. By now they had reached the top of the stairs. "It's coming from behind that door," she said. Holding her breath, Deena forced herself to tiptoe toward the room.

She reached out and pushed the door open.

It was a bedroom, with a big four-poster bed and two large bureaus. Against the far wall a casement window hung open. With every gust of wind it swung back and forth, making the weird creaking noise.

"This house is too spooky," Jade observed from the doorway.

"This is one spook I'm going to put an end to," said Deena. She crossed to the window, nearly slipping in a puddle of rainwater that had blown into the room. "The good news is that it's stopped raining," she told Jade.

"What's the bad news?" said Jade.

"I can't get the window shut," said Deena. "It's stuck against a branch. There's a huge tree right outside."

"Let me help," said Jade. She came over and pushed against the overgrown branch of a big maple tree while Deena pulled the window shut.

"Good work," said Deena. "That sound was making me crazy!" She swung the flashlight around the room. "Think we'll find anything in here?" she said.

"There's nothing in the closet," Jade's muffled voice reported. "Just a bunch of women's clothes. It all smells like mothballs."

The next room was smaller than the first, and as soon as they opened the door Deena knew they'd hit the jackpot. "This has to be his study," she said with growing excitement.

"Great!" Jade said, her voice beginning to show some of her old excitement. In front of the window stood an old metal desk, its top covered with papers. A two-drawer file cabinet was set in the corner, its drawers standing open and empty, while across from the desk was a daybed, also heaped high with papers.

Several boxes and green plastic trash bags sat in disarray, stuffed with papers and files.

"Looks as if Mr. Farberson's clearing out his files," said Jade, sounding satisfied.

"But it could take weeks to go through this stuff," said Deena, "and we don't even know what we're looking for."

"We probably don't have to go through it all," said Jade. "Just skim through the things on top. That's probably the stuff that he's been looking at most recently. You take the couch, and I'll look at the things on the desk."

Deena sat on the couch and began to look through the stacks of files piled there. She flipped through several file folders, most containing receipts for household bills, old income tax forms, and check stubs. She was about to move on when her eye fell on a piece of paper folded and unfolded so many times it was fragile enough to fall apart at a touch. "I think I've found something," she told Jade.

"That makes one of us," said Jade. "What is it?"

"A letter," said Deena. "From Mrs. Farberson to Mr. Farberson. Listen to this!

" 'Dear Stan,' " Deena read. " 'There's no use arguing anymore. I have made up my mind to leave you, and nothing will change that. I know you can't make a go of the restaurant. When I gave you the money to buy it I believed that finally you would be successful at something. But once again you are failing.

" 'I refuse to give you any more money. In the last five years you have gone through almost all of my inheritance. I have to save something for myself.

" 'I'll be by Saturday night to pick up my things. Good-bye, Edna.' "

"That's it!" said Jade. "That's why he killed her. She had money, and she was leaving him."

"It's sort of sad, though," said Deena. "It sounds as if she once really cared about him."

"Which was obviously a big mistake," said Jade. "Anyway, we've got what we came for. Let's get out of here."

"Okay," said Deena. "Just give me a minute. I want to check the closet."

"What for? We have enough evidence to go to the police—"

"I want to try to find the mask," Deena said.

"Okay," said Jade. "But hurry."

Deena opened the closet and shone the flashlight in. "There's a suitcase here," she said.

"Forget it," said Jade urgently. "I hear a car coming."

"Probably just someone driving by," said Deena. She opened the suitcase to find piles of shirts, socks, and trousers. Slipping her hand down beneath the clothes, she felt around, but there was nothing else. Disappointed, she snapped the suitcase shut and began to inspect the contents of the shelves.

"The car sounds close," said Jade, sounding nervous. "Come on—forget the mask."

"All right," said Deena. She backed out of the closet and slipped the letter from Mrs. Farberson into the waistband of her sweats.

And froze.

Now she could hear the car, too.

Hear it slow down, then turn into the Farbersons' driveway.

"It can't be him!" Deena whispered. "It's too early!"

The car door opened and slammed shut.

Heavy footsteps began to walk toward the house.

Then there was the sound of a key turning in a lock, and the front door began to creak open.

chapter

21

Both girls stood very still, scarcely breathing. They could hear someone walking around and then saw a sudden glow from a light that had been switched on downstairs.

"We've got to do something," Jade whispered at last.

"Like what?" said Deena. "All we can do is wait. Maybe he just came home to pick something up." She nervously fingered the letter in her waistband.

It was the proof they needed—the proof that would save Chuck. Somehow they had to get it to the police.

But would they be able to leave?

From downstairs they could now hear Mr. Farberson walking toward the kitchen.

"What if he's home for good?" said Jade, echoing Deena's own fears. "Maybe the restaurant closed early. Or maybe he got sick."

"Then we'll just have to wait till he's asleep," Deena said. "There's no reason for him to know we're here. Let's put our rain gear back on, in case we have to hide."

As quietly as possible, Jade tiptoed to the desk and took her raincoat and Deena's poncho from the back of the desk chair where they'd left them. On the way back her foot creaked on a loose board, and both girls held their breath for a moment, but there was no response from downstairs.

"My mom's going to kill me," whispered Jade, struggling into her yellow slicker. "I told her I'd be home by ten."

"Jade, your mom isn't our major problem right now," Deena whispered.

The girls carefully sat down on the edge of the daybed and waited. And waited. Each minute seemed to take an hour. The poncho was hot, and even though the room was chilly, Deena felt a drop of perspiration roll down her back. If only there was some other way to get out of the house!

What was Mr. Farberson doing now? she wondered. There hadn't been a sound from him for a long time.

"I can't stand it," whispered Jade suddenly. "I'm going to see if I can get a peek. Maybe it isn't even Mr. Farberson down there."

Before Deena could protest, Jade slipped out into the hall. A few moments later she came back, her face looking very worried in the dim light. "He's on the couch with his head back," she reported. "He's snoring."

Deena took a deep breath. "Maybe we ought to try to sneak past him," she said. "What do you think?"

Jade nodded. Both girls took big gulps of air, then began to tiptoe down the hall toward the stairway. The wooden floor was very old, and each step caused a creaking that sounded as loud as an ambulance siren to Deena.

They reached the head of the stairs. From down below Deena could hear the muted sounds of Mr. Farberson's snores.

She started down the stairs, Jade right behind her. Now she could see the top of Mr. Farberson's head propped against the back of the sofa.

She took another step.

And the snoring stopped.

Mr. Farberson grunted, then sat up and stretched. He yawned loudly and then leaned back again.

Deena and Jade froze. Then, still as quietly as possible, they turned around and went back up the stairs and down the hall. By the time they got to Mr. Farberson's office Deena's hands were shaking.

She backed into the office, followed by Jade.

And collided with the metal wastebasket.

The wastebasket fell with a clatter. Almost immediately Mr. Farberson growled from downstairs. "What the devil?" he said.

Deena and Jade studied each other with wide, frightened eyes. Quickly Jade turned the wastebasket right side up. "In the closet!" she hissed to Deena.

Now Deena could hear Mr. Farberson's footsteps climbing the stairs. He didn't seem to be in any hurry, but his steps sounded heavy, and she remembered how big he was.

She slipped into the closet, Jade right behind her.

They got as far back in as they could, behind some coats and shirts.

The footsteps came closer; then there was a click, and a sliver of light appeared under the closet door.

"Hello?" mumbled Mr. Farberson. "Is someone here?"

They heard him walk around the office, muttering to himself. Then his footsteps retreated, and they could hear him walking down the hall to check the other room.

He moved around a bit more, and the girls heard a heavy creaking as he settled himself at his desk. For a moment there was no sound, then a bellow broke the silence. "Hey!" Mr. Farberson said out loud. "How'd these drops of water get all over everything?"

Then suddenly a chair scraped back, and heavy footsteps crossed the room.

The closet door swung open.

Deena blinked against the light, unable to see anything, but then she saw Mr. Farberson, his angry face staring directly at her. His expression changed slowly—the anger faded and was replaced by a cruel, mocking smile.

"Well, well, girls," he said. "Just can't stay away, can you?"

chapter

22

Deena was so terrified she couldn't move or think. And then Jade let out an earsplitting scream.

Mr. Farberson stepped back in surprise, and Jade rushed out of the closet, pushing past him. She sprinted across the room, but he was faster and blocked the door with his body.

Deena peeked out of the closet to see Jade standing behind Mr. Farberson's desk, her cheeks flushed and her eyes bright with excitement and fear.

"Let us go!" Jade said. "We know everything about you!"

"I doubt that," he said, not seeming worried at all. He crossed his arms and continued to lean against the door frame.

"We know you're a liar!" Jade went on. "We know you murdered your wife!"

Farberson's eyes narrowed, but then his face relaxed again. "You shouldn't make nasty accusations like that," he said. "Especially not when I just caught you breaking into my house—for the second time!"

"I warn you," Jade went on. "You'd better let us go, or—"

"Or what?" Mr. Farberson said nastily.

Deena helplessly continued to watch, admiring her friend for standing up to Mr. Farberson, but she could see Jade had run out of threats. Quick as a cat, Mr. Farberson grabbed Jade by the wrist.

"Let me go!" she screamed. She picked up an ashtray with her free hand and swung it at Mr. Farberson, but it slipped harmlessly from her fingers and shattered to the floor.

Mr. Farberson grabbed her other wrist, and she screamed again. "So you like to play rough, do you?" he said.

Frantically Deena searched for anything or any way to help her friend. "Let her go!" she yelled. She threw her flashlight at Mr. Farberson, catching him on the shoulder, but he only grunted and held on more tightly to Jade.

Jade tried to scratch and bite Mr. Farberson, but he easily held her off. Suddenly tiring of her, he shook her. "All right!" he said. "Enough playing around! It's time to teach you girls a lesson!" He slammed Jade hard against the desk. She gasped, then screamed again. "Run, Deena! Get help!"

Deena didn't want to leave Jade, but there was no way she could fight Mr. Farberson. She fled from the room and down the stairs. Behind her she could hear Jade and Mr. Farberson continuing to struggle.

At the foot of the stairs she paused a moment,

deciding. Where could she go for help? The nearby houses all seemed to be deserted.

Then her eye fell on the phone. Better to call the cops from here, she thought. She picked up the phone, started to dial . . . and got nothing but dead air. Too late, she remembered that the phone was out.

This had all started with a phone call, she thought. And it might end—because she couldn't make one!

At a heavy footstep she turned to find Mr. Farberson standing right behind her. "Phoning for pizza?" he asked.

Deena stared at him, her heart pounding in her throat.

"Where's Jade?" she asked, backing away.

"Taking a little nap, you might say," said Mr. Farberson. "And I'm sure she'd just love for you to keep her company."

Deena backed up slowly, then on an impulse spun around and sprinted toward the kitchen. But Mr. Farberson was right behind her. Desperately she reached for something—anything—to use as a weapon. Her hand closed on the handle of an iron frying pan, and she gripped it tightly.

Mr. Farberson, his big body in silhouette because of the light behind him, lumbered slowly toward her, his hands outstretched like those of a movie monster.

This is a nightmare, Deena thought. This can't be happening to me!

But she wasn't dreaming, and Mr. Farberson proved it the next instant when he lunged at her. With a little shriek she swung the pan as hard as she could and felt it connect. He let out a bellow of rage and pain, then grabbed the other end of the pan and began to twist. The rough metal cut her fingers, and she had to let go.

Mr. Farberson reached out, grasped her shoulders, and picked her up as easily as if she'd been a doll.

"You little idiot—you cut my hand with that frying pan!" he said. "Who would have thought two girls could cause me so much trouble?"

Deena struggled, but it was no use. She had started to cry and tried to stop but couldn't. He carried her into the living room and set her down at the bottom of the stairs, closing his hand on her arm like a vise. "Come on!" he said. "I don't care if I break your arm."

He started up the stairs, half leading and half dragging her. She had to walk fast to keep her arm from being pulled out of its socket.

In the hall upstairs he stopped in front of the first door she and Jade had opened—the one to the bedroom. He reached in his pocket, searching for a key. The door wasn't locked before, Deena remembered. Was Jade in there? She didn't have time to think about it because just for a moment he let her go while he unlocked the door.

Deena knew this was her last chance.

She began to run down the hall, but Mr. Farberson was fast for such a big man, and he tackled her, throwing her to the floor on her back. She fought as hard as she could, struggling desperately. She heard a ripping noise as Mr. Farberson tore her poncho up the middle and pulled it down so her arms were trapped at her sides.

chapter

23

I'm totally trapped, Deena thought. What is he going to do to me now?

"Hey—what's this?" he said. The torn poncho revealed the letter in her waistband. He snatched it out, and his face grew even angrier. "So!" he said. "This is what you were after!"

Quickly he pulled Deena to her feet and pushed her into the bedroom. Then he followed her in, slammed the door, and stood still for a moment, breathing hard.

Deena had fallen against one of the bureaus. She pulled herself to a sitting position and looked around. Jade was lying crumpled at the foot of the bed. "Jade!" she cried in horror. The still form didn't move. "Jade!" This time Deena screamed it. "You've killed my friend!" she yelled at Mr. Farberson. She was so frightened and angry she could hardly breathe.

"She's just knocked out," he said. "I wouldn't be

148

surprised if she's playing possum. I didn't hit her hard enough to kill her—not yet."

On the bed Jade moaned. Deena struggled with the poncho and finally twisted free of it. Then she went to her friend. A nasty bruise was forming on Jade's forehead, and she was very pale, but after a moment her eyes fluttered open. "Deena?" she said.

"Jade!" cried Deena. "Jade, are you all right?"

"My head hurts," said Jade. "What's happening— oh!" she gasped as she saw Mr. Farberson still standing in front of the door. He was holding the letter in one hand, tapping it against the other, blood dripping from the cut where Deena had hit him.

"He found our proof," said Deena, still crying. "I'm sorry, Jade."

"What I found was a letter that belongs to me," said Mr. Farberson. "Something you girls were trying to steal. I've half a mind to turn you girls over to the police."

For a moment Deena felt a surge of hope. Maybe he wasn't going to do anything terrible to them. Maybe he would just turn them over to the police. At least then they'd be safe.

"Tell me what you *think* you know, girls," Farberson said.

"We don't know anything," Deena said quickly.

"Oh, is that so?" Farberson said, his eyes narrowing. "Hey—I'm not playing games here. Tell me what you think you know." He took a step toward them. "I don't mind hurting you to get the answer!"

"You know already," said Deena, angry again. She felt that Mr. Farberson was playing with them the way a cat plays with a mouse. "You murdered your wife for her money—and tried to make it look like a burglary!"

For a moment Mr. Farberson didn't speak, then he straightened, as if he'd made a decision. "Well, you girls are real smart," he said. "Too smart for your own good. I've got to take care of myself now."

"What do you mean?" whispered Jade.

"I mean maybe you were right—about everything," he said. "Maybe I killed Edna."

Deena felt cold all over. He wouldn't be confessing if he was going to let her and Jade go. The only thing she could think to do was keep him talking, buy time somehow.

"You killed her and convinced the police it was Chuck?" she asked.

A strange smile formed on Farberson's face. "When you three kids showed up that night it was like pennies from heaven. You bought me even more time—time to do what I had to and get away. I'm grateful to you, if you want to know."

"You can still get away," Deena said quickly. "Jade and I won't say anything to anyone till after your plane leaves tomorrow."

"Nice try," said Farberson. "I've thought about it—thought about just leaving you locked up here till it's time to go. But you know too much. I can't take a chance on your stopping me."

"Wait," said Deena. "What about—"

It was too late. Mr. Farberson had backed out the door. "Don't go away now," he said, grinning nastily.

He slammed the door, and Deena heard the key turning in the lock. His footsteps faded down the hall.

chapter

24

*D*eena ran to the door and tried to open it, just in case, but the knob wouldn't turn. "Come on," she said to Jade. "We've got to get out of here!"

"But how?" said Jade.

"That way." Deena pointed to the window. "Remember when I tried to shut the window before? And a branch was in the way? That big old tree is really close to the house—maybe only a couple of feet away."

"Are you saying we should *climb* down?" asked Jade.

"We don't have a choice! Jade, he's going to *kill* us!" She lifted the window latch and began to push, but the window was stuck.

"Hurry, Deena," said Jade. "He's coming back!"

Now Deena could hear Mr. Farberson's footsteps on the stairs, too.

"Why did I ever want to shut this window?" Deena moaned. She pushed as hard as she could, but nothing happened.

"We've got to slow him down!" said Jade breathlessly. "Come help me!" Deena watched as Jade pushed against a heavy chest of drawers. She ran to help her friend. With both girls pushing as hard as they could the heavy object began to move slowly across the floor.

Outside the door the sound of Mr. Farberson's approaching footsteps echoed.

"Hurry!" said Jade again.

The chest moved inch by inch—and stopped against the door just as Mr. Farberson's key slid into the lock.

Deena darted back to work on the window. There was a thumping sound as Mr. Farberson tried to open the door and found the bureau blocking his way.

Deena heard him curse loudly. Then there was a tremendous thud as Mr. Farberson threw himself against the door. The chest moved an inch or two. The door was open far enough now for Mr. Farberson to stick his arm through. "You can't keep me out!" he said from the other side of the door. And he began to laugh—a chilling laugh!

With renewed desperation both girls pushed on the window again, and this time it sprang open. Deena looked out. Four feet below the window was a limb thick enough to hold both girls. The branches near the window were too thin to offer much of a handhold. The tree was still slippery with water.

The bureau gave a sudden lurch. If Mr. Farberson had been any smaller, he could have burst into the room at that moment.

"Move, Deena!" cried Jade, her voice filled with terror. Deena took a deep breath and climbed onto the windowsill. She turned around and, gripping the sill with her fingers, swung out and down. With relief she felt her feet touch the limb below, and she let go of the windowsill, sagging against the trunk. Gratefully she wrapped one arm around the rough bark and held the other out to Jade.

Seconds after Jade joined Deena in the tree Mr. Farberson appeared in the window. "You won't get away!" he snarled, and he immediately disappeared.

"He's coming outside!" Jade whispered. "Quick, climb down!"

Deena looked down and realized they were much higher up than she had thought.

The next branch was just beyond her reach. Why didn't I ever learn gymnastics? she asked herself.

"I can't!" she told Jade. "It's too slippery and too far."

"I'm taller," said Jade. "I'll try. Then if—oh!" Her eyes grew wide with a new fear. In the light from the kitchen window both girls could now see Mr. Farberson walking toward the tree. He was holding something long and bulky, and when he got closer Deena realized that it was a chain saw!

"Oh, no," moaned Jade. "I don't believe it!"

"He can't use a chain saw at night!" Deena said in disbelief. "He'll wake everyone on Fear Street. Is he crazy?"

"Yes," Jade whispered. "Yes, he is. I mean, he's gone over the edge. Just look at his eyes."

Deena squinted down and saw what Jade meant. Mr. Farberson's face still looked mean and angry. But now there was something else there—a wildness that revealed he was out of control. The whites of his eyes were huge in the dim light. Once again he let out a terrifying laugh. Deena shivered. Somehow this new Mr. Farberson was even scarier than the man who'd been threatening them.

He started to rev up the saw.

Just before the deafening roar blotted out all other sound Deena thought she heard a high-pitched wail.

The tree began to vibrate as Mr. Farberson cut into it with the power saw. Deena and Jade held on to the trunk as tightly as they could to keep from being shaken off—and into the whirling blades of the chain saw.

"He'll saw right through it in no time!" Deena cried, almost slipping off the branch.

"We're going to fall!" Jade said, looking down.

Down below Farberson pulled back the saw, revved it up again, and, glaring up at the girls, returned the blade to the tree.

The saw made a deafening grinding sound as it ate deeper into the tree. Sawdust and wood chips flew all around.

Deena heard a cracking sound. "We're going down!" she cried.

chapter

25

*S*uddenly Jade grabbed Deena's arm. "Look!" She mouthed the word. Deena turned her head.

There, in the distance, coming from the direction of the Mill Road, was the most beautiful sight she had ever seen: the flashing red lights of police cars!

Another cracking sound. The tree began to tilt.

Help was on the way, but would it arrive in time?

In the next instant everything seemed to happen at once.

The tree tilted even farther. Deena closed her eyes and held tightly to the trunk, expecting each moment to be her last.

Then suddenly the yard filled with an eerie, flashing glow as police cars pulled up to the house. A police officer ran across the lawn, his gun out in front of him. With relief, Deena recognized Detective Frazier.

His gun flashed once, then twice more. Mr. Farberson stood stock-still, then jerked backward and fell, the chain saw still roaring in his hands. Quickly the detective ran to Farberson and shut the machine off.

The relief from the noise and vibration was startling—and in the sudden silence Deena wondered for a moment if she had gone deaf.

"You girls okay?" Detective Monroe was under the tree, peering up at them. Behind him Detective Frazier and a uniformed policeman were bent over Mr. Farberson.

"Try not to move," Monroe said. "I'll get a ladder."

Deena was so relieved she felt weak all over. She looked at Jade and could see she felt the same way. Both girls were crying tears of relief, and it was only when the tree swayed again that Deena realized they were still in trouble.

The yard was now filled with the voices of shouting men, the sounds of motors running and radios squawking. Through the dense leaves Deena could see someone speaking into a walkie-talkie, and beyond him— could it be?—her father and Chuck!

Detective Monroe had arrived with a tall stepladder, and he climbed it while a uniformed policeman held it steady. He reached out for Deena first. Gratefully she put her arms around his neck and relaxed as he carried her down the ladder. A minute later he returned with Jade. Just as he was setting her on the ground someone shouted, "Look out!"

Slowly at first, then more quickly, the tree toppled to the ground, its long branches smashing into the ground-floor windows in the back of Mr. Farberson's house.

Deena looked at it for a moment, her heart thudding in her chest, and then she passed out.

chapter

26

When Deena woke up a few minutes later she was lying on someone's coat on Mr. Farberson's porch. Next to her Jade was sitting cross-legged, holding a cloth to her forehead. And next to *her* Chuck was hunkered down, gazing at Jade with a tender smile.

Deena struggled to a sitting position, then looked around, not believing her eyes. Detectives Frazier and Monroe, three uniformed cops, and her father were all gathered around the porch, staring at her and Jade.

"How are you, sweetheart?" asked her father. He leaned down and gave her a quick hug.

"Daddy!" she said. "And Chuck! What happened?"

Chuck grinned his goofy grin at her. "It's kind of a long story," he said.

"Where's Mr. Farberson?" Deena asked them.

"Over there," said Frazier, pointing to the side yard. "He's wounded, but he'll probably recover—to stand trial." He leaned back on the porch railing and crossed his arms. "It looks as if you girls have quite a story to tell," he said. "While we're waiting for an ambulance, why don't you tell us what you're doing here?"

"We were trying to find out what we could about Mr. Farberson," Deena said.

"And what did you find out?" Frazier's face was blank, and Deena had no idea what he was thinking.

"He killed his wife," said Jade. "He did it for her money."

"You're sure of this?" said Frazier. Beside him Detective Monroe had started to take notes.

"Look in Mr. Farberson's pocket!" said Deena. "He has a letter from his wife saying she was leaving him. And he has plane reservations to South America."

"Besides," said Jade, "he told us he did it." Deena noticed that Jade's voice was no longer dull, but strong, and that her face had some of the old sparkle in it.

"You say Farberson told you he killed his wife," said Frazier. "Did he happen to mention why?" His voice sounded faintly sarcastic, and Deena suddenly felt angry.

"His wife had a lot of money," Deena said, her voice showing how she felt. "She wasn't going to let him have any more of it. Besides, he was having an affair with his assistant, Linda Morrison."

"Just how did you girls come by all this information?" Frazier asked, turning back to the porch.

"We looked for it!" said Jade, sounding bitter. "We went to where Mr. Farberson worked, and to Miss Morrison's house, and then we came here!"

"You took an awful chance!" said Frazier. "Don't you think that was a job for the police?"

"Of course it was!" said Deena. "But you wouldn't listen to anything we said. We knew Chuck was innocent, and we knew his only hope was for us to find out the truth."

To Deena's surprise, Frazier smiled. "I guess I should tell you, Farberson has been our number-one suspect for some time," he said. "We've just been waiting till we could get proof."

"You've been w-waiting—" Deena stammered. "But what about Chuck? All this time you've had him locked up!"

"Take it easy, Deena," said Chuck. "It's okay."

"How can it be okay?" protested Deena. "If the police knew all along that you were innocent, how could they have—"

"We didn't know for sure," Detective Frazier interrupted. "You see, Farberson was clever to involve you kids. Finding Chuck's prints on the knife threw us off at first. But then we started watching Farberson. We didn't have any evidence, and we didn't want him to know he was a suspect."

"You kept my brother in jail for a week just to help your investigation?" Deena was so angry she felt like throwing something.

"Hey, Deena, take it easy," said Chuck. "Let Detective Monroe explain."

"No, I'll explain," said Mr. Martinson. Deena studied her father, wondering if everyone had gone crazy.

"My lawyer arranged to get Chuck out on bail on Wednesday," Deena's father said. "But Detective Frazier explained the situation to me. He told me there was a better chance of arresting Farberson if he continued to think Chuck was the main suspect."

"And you *agreed?*" Deena remembered how Chuck had looked when she visited him in jail. How desperate, and how frightened. Now, suddenly, she was furious at her father. As furious as she was at the detectives.

Mr. Martinson looked embarrassed and shrugged. "It was only for a couple of days," he said. "Chuck would have gotten out tomorrow anyway. I wanted to help the police. And—I thought it might teach Chuck a lesson."

"It's okay, Dad," Chuck said. "I think I understand." He had one hand on the back of Jade's neck, and Deena thought he was a different person from the boy who had come to Shadyside less than three weeks earlier. His face looked older, more serious. All traces of the bitter sneer had disappeared.

An ambulance sped down Fear Street then and turned into the driveway. Detectives Frazier and Monroe went over to assist the paramedics. Deena and Jade watched as they loaded Mr. Farberson onto a stretcher and then put him in the ambulance.

"I can't believe it's *over*," said Deena.

"Believe it," said Chuck. "Thanks to everything you and Jade did, the police know the truth. They know I'm innocent—and they have the evidence against Farberson to put him in jail for life."

The ambulance backed out of the driveway and sped back to the Mill Road, its red lights blinking. The

police experts all seemed to have finished their work
and were starting to pack up.

"Do you need us for anything else?" Mr. Martinson
asked Detective Frazier.

"No, go on home," said the detective. "But I'
want to talk to the girls again tomorrow."

"Fine. Ready, girls?"

Deena pulled herself to her feet. "You bet," she
said, and then she stopped and turned back to Detective Frazier. "There's just one thing I don't understand," she said.

"What's that?" said Detective Frazier.

"Nobody knew where we were. How did you ge
here in time to save us?"

"You've got Chuck to thank for that," said Detective Frazier. "He tried to call your parents and te
them what you girls were planning, but he couldn't ge
through. So he finally called me at home—and said h
wanted to confess."

"You *what?*" said Jade and Deena together, staring
at Chuck.

Chuck just grinned his goofy grin. "I had to see hin
as soon as possible," he said. "It was the only way
could be sure he'd listen to me."

Deena and Jade stared at each other, then back a
Chuck. Jade started laughing. "I don't believe you di
that, Chuck!" she said, gasping. "After everything
you promised, after everything we've all bee
through . . ."

"What are you talking about?" said Chuck, looking
puzzled.

"I just mean," said Jade, still laughing, "that you—
you made another prank phone call!"

chapter
27

*M*onday in school, no one could talk about anything but what had happened. There had been only a brief article in the paper about Mr. Farberson's arrest, but somehow word got out that Deena, Chuck, and Jade had all been involved. By lunchtime the gossip had turned them all into heroes.

When Deena went to her locker before lunch she found a traffic jam. It seemed that everyone in school wanted the juicy details.

"Congratulations, Deena!" said Della O'Connor.

"Did you really help the police solve a murder?" Cory Brooks wanted to know.

"Okay, everyone, take a number!" Deena cracked. At that moment Lisa Blume came up, her notebook ready. "Good morning, Deena," she said. "You must feel great!"

"I'm just glad it's all over," Deena said truthfully.

"I'm ready to write that exclusive," Lisa said.

"Can we talk after school?" Deena said. "I'm starving."

"Well, can you just tell me if it's true that your brother made a fake confession?" Lisa persisted.

"Here he comes now," said Deena, banging her locker shut. "Why don't you ask him yourself?"

Now Chuck came around the corner, holding hands with Jade. Jade was wearing one of her fabulous multicolored outfits, and she looked gorgeous. She was smiling at Chuck as if she'd never let him out of her sight.

Lisa pounced immediately, and Deena was surprised to see Chuck grin and start answering her questions.

Deena started to walk over to Jade when she saw Rob Morell walking toward her.

"Hey, how's it goin'?" he said with a big smile.

"Hi, Rob," she said, too surprised to feel shy.

"I tried to call you this weekend," he said. "Now I know why you didn't answer."

She just smiled at him, not knowing what to say.

"The thing is," Rob went on, "some of the gang are coming over to my house to watch some tapes. I'd like it if you'd come, too."

"I'd—I'd like to very much," Deena said, her heart pounding.

"Great," said Rob. "I'll pick you up around seven. And you, too," he added to Chuck and Jade. "Come on over."

"Thanks," said Jade, "I might have too much

164

homework tonight. I'll let you know later. Deena, I'll give you a call after school."

"Okay," said Deena. She started to turn down the hall, then stopped. "On second thought," she told Jade, "I think I've had it with telephones for a while. Maybe you should just send me a postcard!"

About the Author

R. L. STINE is the author of more than 70 books of humor, adventure, and mystery for young readers. In recent years, he has been concentrating on scary thrillers, such as this one.

For ten years, he was editor of *Bananas*, a national humor magazine for young people. In addition to magazine and book writing, he is currently Head Writer of the children's TV show, "Eureeka's Castle."

He lives in New York City with his wife Jane and son Matthew.

THE NIGHTMARES
NEVER END . . .
WHEN YOU VISIT

NEXT: *THE SLEEPWALKER*

The terror begins late one night when Mayra
wakes up in her nightgown in the middle of the
Fear Street woods. Why has she begun to
sleepwalk? Has the mysterious old woman she
works for cast a spell on her? Mayra knows she
has to find the answer soon—before she
sleepwalks to her death!

FEAR STREET®

R.L. Stine